He was not supposed to be falling for Deborah Mast.

He ordered two double dips of ice cream, getting a variety of flavors since he had no idea what she liked. Passing the money to the teen working the cash register, he noticed his hand shaking slightly.

Get a grip, man.

Pulling in a deep breath, he accepted the change, tossed it into the tip jar and carried the ice cream to Deborah.

"Mint chocolate chip with strawberry? Interesting combination…"

"Uh, *ya.* Or you could have this one…" He thrust the second cone toward her.

She stepped closer to him, accepted the mystery ice cream and took a bite. "Buttered pecan on top, and I'm pretty sure that's chocolate chip on bottom. Pretty *gut* too."

He could not be falling for this woman. She was all wrong for him. She was independent and strong-willed and the *mamm* of two boys.

She was beautiful and made him laugh.

But most importantly, she was everything that his five-year plan did not allow for.

Vannetta Chapman has published over one hundred articles in Christian family magazines and received over two dozen awards from Romance Writers of America chapter groups. She discovered her love for the Amish while researching her grandfather's birthplace of Albion, Pennsylvania. Her first novel, *A Simple Amish Christmas*, quickly became a bestseller. Chapman lives in Texas Hill Country with her husband.

Books by Vannetta Chapman

Love Inspired

Indiana Amish Brides

Visit the Author Profile page at LoveInspired.com.

The Amish Twins Next Door

Vannetta Chapman

LOVE INSPIRED
INSPIRATIONAL ROMANCE

LOVE INSPIRED®
INSPIRATIONAL ROMANCE

PLEASE RECYCLE
THIS PRODUCT IS RECYCLABLE

Recycling programs for this product may not exist in your area.

ISBN-13: 978-1-335-75921-4

The Amish Twins Next Door

Love Inspired
22 Adelaide St. West, 41st Floor
Toronto, Ontario M5H 4E3, Canada
www.LoveInspired.com

Printed in U.S.A.

Lo, children are an heritage of the Lord.
—*Psalm* 127:3

This book is dedicated to Professor Audrey Wick.

Chapter One

June 1

Deborah Mast stood on the front porch, worrying her thumbnail. How long had it been since she'd seen the boys? Ten minutes? Fifteen? What was worse, she couldn't hear them. As long as they were close enough to be within earshot, she didn't worry. But when silence descended upon the land, more often than not, that indicated trouble.

Double trouble.

No one had told her what raising twins would be like, and of course she hadn't expected to be a single parent. But there you had it. Life often did not turn out as you would expect.

She stepped off the porch.

Too quiet.

Something was up.

Circling the house, she checked the trampoline and swing set. They weren't at either of those places. Picking up her pace, she headed to the barn, but the door was firmly shut and latched.

Where else could they be?

Her *dat* was inside the house, so they weren't helping him.

Her *mamm* was cooking dinner, and they most certainly weren't helping her.

Then she heard it—a male shout, followed by Joseph's concerned voice and Jacob's peal of laughter. *Uh-oh.* She hurried toward the property line separating her parents' place from the new neighbor's.

Nicholas Stoltzfus had recently purchased the adjacent farm. Her father had spoken with the man several times, but Deborah hadn't yet met him. She knew he'd been raised in the area, had lived in Maine for ten years and had recently moved back. She also knew he was a bachelor, which meant he'd receive a lot of interest from the single girls in their community. At twenty-five, Deborah no longer considered herself a part of that particular group. True, she was single—as her *mamm* loved to point out—but she wasn't exactly on the prowl for a man. She had her hands full with Jacob and Joseph.

Breaking through the line of maple trees, she stopped in her tracks, hand pressing her side where a stitch had developed from running. The fingers of her other hand went to her lips in an attempt to hold in her laughter.

Jacob was standing on the fence rail, a fishing pole held in both his hands. Joseph had scrambled through to the other side and was attempting to catch the cattle dog that had apparently been hooked through his collar. And then there was the neighbor—tall, handsome and not amused.

She rushed over, admonishing Jacob to drop the fishing rod.

"But then he'll get away," her son protested.

"Drop it!"

The dog, realizing he was no longer being reeled in

by a six-year-old, took off running toward his owner, dragging the rod behind him. Joseph threw himself at the dog and the reel and managed to get his arms around both.

"Hold on, boy. We'll set you free. Just hold on."

Even in her hurry to reach them, Deborah noticed how gentle Joseph was with the dog. He stopped to look in the dog's eyes and scratch behind his ears, then freed him from the fishing line.

"See. It's all okay. You're fine."

"It is *not* all okay." Nicholas Stoltzfus reached Joseph and the dog at the same time that Deborah did. "You could have hurt my dog. You could have taken out an eye with that fishing hook. What were you thinking?"

"Not possible." Jacob hopped off the fence and joined them, thumbs under his suspenders, straw hat pushed back on his head. "Wasn't using a hook. Just a small weight."

"The weight could have hit him in the eye."

"Oh." Jacob cocked his head to the side and studied the dog. "I didn't think of that. But how are we supposed to practice without a weight?"

"Practice on your own property."

"Technically, we were on our property…"

"Jacob, watch your tongue." Deborah stepped forward, though she was still on their side of the fence.

"But, *Mamm*…"

The look she gave him silenced his protests. He dropped to the ground and proceeded to smother the poor dog with affection—apologizing, assuring the beast that they meant no harm, complimenting him on his mottled coat and dark ears. Looking down at her sons, at their red heads touching as they played with the dog, Deborah couldn't hold back her smile. They were rambunctious and didn't always think things through, but what six-year-old did? They had compassionate hearts. That was what mattered most to her.

"I would think you'd take this more seriously."

"What?" She jerked her head up in surprise. "I'm sorry, we haven't met. I'm Deborah Mast. We live…"

"John's *doschder*, *ya*, I guessed. If you could keep your boys on your side of the fence…"

"Jacob and Joseph, stand up and say hello to our new neighbor. This is Nick."

"Nicholas," the man practically growled.

"Nicholas." Deborah attempted to smile her apology, but the man seemed intent on ignoring her. "Remember, your *daddi* mentioned him at dinner last night."

Both boys popped up and extended a small hand.

Nicholas shook them, then quickly stuck his hands in his pockets and took a step back. He was only a few inches taller than Deborah, maybe five foot eight, and slightly built. His hair was a light brown, and his face might be good-looking if he ever smiled. His dark brown eyes were set off by frown lines. This guy was a worrier, no doubt about that.

"Howdy." Joseph sent another longing look toward the dog. "What's his name?"

"Blue."

"But he's white and black and brown."

"He's a blue heeler. That's why I named him Blue."

Deborah barely resisted laughing at that. It seemed their neighbor was bad-tempered, inexperienced with children and wholly unimaginative. He named his blue heeler dog Blue? Did he name his chestnut mare Chestnut? Deborah only knew she was a chestnut mare because her *dat* had mentioned that he'd bought her from Old Tim and managed to talk him down on the price.

Few people were successful negotiating Old Tim down. It usually wasn't worth the time involved.

Her neighbor was miserly, bad-tempered, inexperienced and unimaginative. Plus, he was older than she'd expected. Was that gray hair at his temples?

"Seems like a *gut* farm dog." Jacob kicked the toe of his shoe in the dirt, no doubt imitating what he'd seen the older boys do at their church gatherings. "Are you planning on more animals? I guess Blue would make a *gut* work dog, if you are planning to bring in cattle or goats. Me and Joseph, we want a dog, but *Mamm* says we're not responsible enough yet."

"As evidenced by the fishing line you managed to tangle around Blue." Nicholas crossed his arms and frowned at the boys.

"That was a *gut* cast, huh? I told Joseph I could do it, but he was worried we'd get in trouble. We're not in trouble, are we?"

Instead of answering that question, Nicholas addressed Deborah. "I'd appreciate it if you could keep your boys…"

"Jacob. My name's Jay—cob. And this is Jo—seph." Jacob spoke with slow exaggeration, but clamped his mouth shut when Deborah gave him *the look*.

She studied Nicholas a minute, then turned to her boys. "Home, both of you, now. Wash up and set the table for *Mammi*."

"Race you," Jacob said.

And then he was gone. Joseph paused to give Blue one last hug and then trotted off in his *bruder*'s wake.

Deborah waited until they were out of earshot.

"You're not fond of children, I take it."

"I wouldn't say that."

Deborah held up both hands. "I get it. I wasn't terribly fond of them myself until I had two. Actually, I rather avoided children in general. Since I'm the youngest in my family, that was fairly easy to do. But now…"

Nicholas looked as if he wanted to ask what had changed, but to give him credit, he kept that rather intrusive question to himself.

"I'll certainly speak with my boys and remind them to respect our boundary line."

"Danki."

"But I have to warn you that they are boys, not yet seven, and they often forget what they're told."

"Maybe you should take a stronger hand with them."

"Is that so?" Deborah wished she could work up the energy to be offended, but she was too used to people telling her how to raise her sons. She was worn down to the point of simply ignoring and shrugging off such comments. "And you know that after spending ten minutes with them?"

"Well…" Nicholas nodded toward the dog, who was now lying with his head on his paws, staring after the boys. "If today was any indication, then yes."

"Your dog isn't hurt."

"But he could have been."

"They weren't even using a hook."

"If that sinker were to hit him in the eye, we'd be on the way to the vet's right now."

"I suspect Jacob did not cast that line with the strength of a major-league pitcher." Deborah wasn't exactly perturbed, but she wasn't pleased, either. Nicholas Stoltzfus seemed to be an irritating know-it-all. "I will remind Jacob and Joseph to stay on our side of the property."

"That's all I ask."

"But if they should forget…" She paused, waited for

him to contradict her again and was profoundly glad when he didn't. "Simply send them back."

"Send them back?"

"Sure. Like a letter put in your mailbox that doesn't belong there. Return to sender."

"Fine."

"Fine." She plastered on an overly bright smile. "It was nice meeting you."

It wasn't, but she had to say something.

Nicholas, on the other hand, only nodded, though his scowl became more pronounced.

Deborah walked home slowly, enjoying the last of the day's light, savoring the moments of quiet. The first day of June brought with it a myriad of feelings for her. She enjoyed the longer days and warm sunshine. Summer would bring her sons' birthday, and in the fall they would begin school. How was she old enough to have children in school? June also brought with it a decision she needed to make—she'd promised her parents that she'd begin dating this summer. The boys were old enough to understand that it made sense for her to find someone and to marry. They were old enough to want a stepfather. Why did she find that thought so distasteful?

She loved her boys more than the air that she breathed, though she understood that they could be a handful. But children were a gift. They helped you see the world in a new light. They reminded you of *Gotte*'s love, of the joy in providing for others through a hard day's work. At least once a day, she would look at Jacob and Joseph and commit herself to leaving this world better than she'd found it.

An image of their new neighbor popped into her mind.

She was fairly certain that Nicholas Stoltzfus wouldn't

agree with any of those things. He seemed quite intent on being left alone. She wished him good luck with that, but something told her that he hadn't seen the last of her twins.

Nick was sitting at the kitchen table eating an egg and toast for dinner when his younger *bruder* stopped by.

David dropped into a chair across from him and shook his head in mock consternation. "Why do you live this way, Nick?"

He grunted but didn't answer. He was thinking of the way he'd corrected Deborah when she'd called him Nick. He must have sounded like a real jerk, but he didn't care. He didn't want her to feel familiar, to feel casual around him. He had no intention of becoming friends with the neighbor's *doschder*, or any other woman, for that matter.

Once burned, twice shy, as his *mamm* liked to say.

"You really should come eat at our place."

"And miss my own excellent cooking?" He sopped up the last of the egg yolk, popped the bread into his mouth and then stood to refill his coffee mug. Waving the pot at his *bruder*, he asked, "Want some?"

"Caffeinated?"

"*Nein*. It's six in the evening. Who drinks caffeinated coffee in the evening?"

"Parents. We need it if we're going to outlast the young ones."

David had three children, though he'd only been married four years. He and Lydia seemed intent on setting some Amish record for having the most children in the least amount of time. Looking in the refrigerator, Nick retrieved a soda for his *bruder*, who then guzzled half of it.

"Speaking of kids…"

"Were we?"

"I met the neighbor's *doschder* and her twin boys today."

"Deborah. *Ya*. She and Lydia know each other, even visit occasionally."

Nick felt his eyebrow arch. "The boys, they're quite the handful."

"What children aren't? I can't imagine having twins and raising them alone. That can't be easy."

"What's the story there?"

"Story?"

"They're redheaded with freckles, so…"

"Ah. Right. I guess it's not gossiping since everyone knows, and Deborah doesn't attempt to hide it."

"Hide what?"

David shrugged. "Her past. Her sins or mistakes or whatever."

Nick told himself that he wasn't interested in either, but he waited for his *bruder* to continue.

"Nothing you haven't heard before. She dated an *Englischer* when she was eighteen or nineteen, I guess. She'd been living with an *aenti* over in Sugarcreek."

"Ohio?"

"That's the only Sugarcreek I'm aware of." David downed the rest of the soda, stood and dropped the can into the recycle bin under the sink.

"And then?"

"Then what?"

"What happened in Sugarcreek?"

"Oh. *Ya*. Well, I suppose they became engaged, she

planned to switch over to the Mennonite faith, then became pregnant and the fella ditched her."

"Ditched her?"

"I'm not clear on that part. You could ask Lydia, though. Deborah doesn't make any bones about it. I think she views it as a cautionary tale for our *youngies*."

"The father has nothing to do with them?" Nick didn't want children. He didn't understand children. Honestly, they terrified him. But he couldn't imagine ignoring his responsibility to any that were his own. Not that he'd ever get caught in such a situation.

"I think Lydia mentioned he had signed over his parental rights, then joined a punk band and moved to Chicago."

Sounded like an *Englisch* soap opera to Nick, not that he'd ever watched one.

"When did all this happen?"

David laughed. "In the last seven years, obviously. Must have been when you were living in Maine."

That made sense. She had to be ten years younger than him, so it wasn't as if they would have been in school at the same time. Still, he was surprised that he didn't remember her at all.

"When she moved back, she spoke in front of our congregation—a confession of sorts, though the bishop didn't require that. She simply wanted to stop the gossip and set the record straight. She was baptized and formally joined the church. The boys were infants then."

"Those two boys are a handful. They need a father in their lives."

"You volunteering?" David grinned at him and leaned back in the chair, his arms crossed.

"I am not."

"Oh. Well, you know the saying…lead, follow or get out of the way."

"I have no intention of being in the way."

"Sounds like it won't be a problem, then."

But as David drove away, Nick found himself thinking not of the boys. No, he was thinking of Deborah Mast.

Her laughing brown eyes.

The way she looked at him with barely disguised amusement.

She was young, and he supposed some would find her good-looking—blond hair, a nice figure and a fabulous smile. Surely she could find a husband if she was willing to try. No one would hold her past against her— at least, he didn't think eligible men in their community would. A mistake made was just that—a mistake. She had come back and rejoined the fold.

So why was she single and living on her parents' place?

And how was he going to keep a healthy distance between himself and the family? He'd already agreed to raise goats with her *dat*. Though he wasn't quite old enough to retire and hand the farm over to a son, John Mast had suffered a stroke the previous year. His left side hadn't fully recovered. He'd offered to provide half the grazing land and pay for all the feed if Nicholas would handle the daily care of the goats.

He sank into his front porch rocker and groaned.

He'd gone to Maine to find adventure, had fallen in love there and had his heart broken by the woman he was certain would be his *fraa*. That had ended in disaster and hurt feelings. He simply wasn't good with women, and he certainly wasn't good with children.

But goats he knew.

Goats he could raise, and he could raise them well.

The only problem was how to do so in partnership with his neighbor—without getting involved with a spunky Amish mom and her two rowdy boys.

Because the one thing he knew for certain was that he wasn't going to risk having his heart broken again. He'd barely survived the last fiasco, and he had learned from his mistake. He was single and alone. He liked it that way. He'd do whatever needed to be done to keep a *gut* distance from the family next door—even if it meant that he came across as rude.

Chapter Two

Deborah kept a close eye on her boys the next two days. When they were outside, she took out her knitting and sat where she could see them. When they walked to the pond at the back of their property, she walked with them. They were old enough to do some things on their own, but they were also fascinated with the new neighbor and his dog, Blue. Hopefully that attention would transfer to something else soon. Until then, she planned to make sure they gave Nicholas Stoltzfus a wide berth.

The last thing she wanted was for her boys to show up on Nicholas's place only to be *sent back*, as if they were a letter delivered to the wrong address. That particular choice of words had been hers, but they had perfectly captured her neighbor's attitude toward her sons.

And her sons weren't the only ones interested in Nicholas Stoltzfus. Her *mamm* had come to the conclusion that *Gotte* had put him next door specifically to court Deborah.

"Where would you get that idea?" They were in the kitchen cleaning up breakfast dishes. The boys were sweeping the front porch. Deborah could hear the low murmur of their voices.

"I've prayed on it, Deborah."

She barely managed to stifle a groan—not this again. "*Mamm*, I know you mean well, but…"

"But what? We've spoken of this before. You can't hide out here forever."

"I'm not hiding."

"It's time for you to date."

"Our neighbor? He's barely moved in and you want me to ask him out on a date?"

"You're doing a *gut* job with Jacob and Joseph."

"Nice to hear." She scrubbed particularly hard on the skillet they'd cooked eggs in. "But…"

"But those boys deserve a *mamm* and *dat*."

Deborah dropped the steel wool into the soapy water, dried her hands on a towel and turned to her mother. Bethany Mast was a dear, wise and stubborn woman. Once she set her mind to something, she could resemble a dog with a bone. Blue popped into Deborah's mind, but she pushed the image away.

Putting a hand on each of her mother's shoulders, she waited until her *mamm* met her eyes. "He doesn't even like children."

"He doesn't know any."

"He's not interested."

"How do you know that?"

"And I'm not ready." She turned back to the dishes, searched in the sudsy water for the steel wool and resumed scrubbing.

"It's frightening, I know."

"How do you know? You've only ever been in love with *Dat*. He's never hurt you in the way that Gavin hurt me."

"You're right, and you're also wrong." Her *mamm* reached for the skillet and dried it. "Your *dat* is the only man I've ever loved, but every marriage—every relationship—has its joys and also its hurts. I might not be able to understand exactly what you went through, but I understand what it feels like to have a bruised heart."

Her *mamm*'s response was so achingly honest that Deborah didn't know what to say. Her *mamm* took the pause as an opportunity to push on.

"You promised us that when the boys were older, you'd begin courting again, and we're going to hold you to that. It's time, Deborah. Stop looking as if I'm insisting you swallow castor oil. Courting is supposed to be a joyful time."

"Right."

"And if you don't want to step out with the neighbor, that's your choice."

"Danki." Relief flooded through Deborah. At least her *mamm* was willing to be reasonable.

"I have a list."

"A what?"

"A list of eligible men."

"Oh, *Mamm*…"

"We can go over it after dinner tonight."

Deborah suddenly needed to be outside. She muttered something about checking on the boys and darted out the door. Why were her parents pushing this? She was happy enough on her own, and the boys were flourishing on the farm.

Things were going quite well, other than their initial fascination with Nicholas Stoltzfus, which seemed to have faded. She could almost believe they'd forgotten about the neighbor and the dog, but then later that afternoon, the goats arrived. Her *dat* went over to watch the unloading, and of course he invited Jacob and Joseph to go with him.

Deborah remembered her promise to keep the boys away from Nicholas's property. Then she blushed thinking of the conversation with her *mamm*.

But she was rather interested in seeing the new animals herself. Technically they half owned them, though how did you own half a goat? Still, she wanted to see. If that irritated Nicholas, it was his problem.

Besides, who could resist a baby goat? Possibly they were all grown, but even an adult goat could be fun to watch. She needed a break from weeding the garden, and it was a bright, warm, sunshiny kind of day.

She popped into the house to check on her *mamm*. "Want to go next door?"

"*Nein.* I believe I'll sit in this chair and enjoy a mug of tea." Bethany Mast was fifty-eight years old and thirty pounds over the weight the doctor insisted she aim for, with a pleasant personality. She also had the faith of a biblical warrior. Still, the last year, in particular the last three months, had worn her down. Since her husband's stroke, she'd seemed to bow under the weight of things. Now, she smiled at Deborah and said, "Go. The boys will love it."

"Promise me you won't start dinner. It's my turn to cook."

"Promise."

She'd barely stepped out of the room when her *mamm* called her back.

"Think about what I said."

Ugh. She was not going to let this courting idea go.

Deborah hurried out the door, practically running to catch up with her *dat* and the boys. Her *dat* was a big man—five foot ten and strong like an ox—but the stroke he'd suffered had affected his left side. His leg, his arm, even his smile was a bit crooked now. The stroke had slowed him down, though no one wanted to admit that. He now walked with a limp, which in turn caused his hip to ache. He never spoke about it, didn't complain at all, but Deborah could tell. When you grew up with someone, you knew them in ways that were hard to describe.

She knew her *dat* was not happy that the stroke had forced him to give up plans to raise goats, or plant the back field, or make a fort for the boys. Those plans had been put on hold—except for the goats, a venture he'd successfully roped Nicholas into sharing. She finally caught up with the little group, and they made their way toward the fence line, the boys dashing out in front of them.

"It'll be *gut* for Jacob and Joseph to help with the goats." Her *dat*'s voice was low, a true baritone that she could easily pick out during their Sunday morning hymn singings.

"Help?"

"Sure. If there's a weakness in a fence, a goat will find it."

"I don't think the boys are able to put up fence quite yet."

"But they can walk it, check for weak points—they only need to be shown what to look for." He waved toward Nicholas's property. "Three-sided, roofed housing is also important. Goats need a dry place to stay out of the weather. Jacob and Joseph could help with building shelters."

"I didn't realize you knew so much about goats." Deborah threaded her arm through her *dat*'s.

He patted her hand, then continued. "They also get

bored easily, and a bored goat is a problem goat. The boys should be able to come up with some play equipment for them."

"*Dat*, they're only six years old."

"I'm aware. You were six when you started helping with your *mamm*'s chickens."

Deborah had forgotten about that. Those chickens had been more important to her than any baby doll. She'd fairly jumped out of bed every morning, needing to check on them herself before leaving for school. It was hard to believe her boys were now that same age.

She recognized the wisdom in what her *dat* was saying, but somehow, she didn't think that Nicholas would agree.

He'd stopped by the day before to speak with her father, but he found an excuse not to come inside. He didn't even step up on the porch, as if the boys might pop out of the house and launch themselves at him. That thought made her smile. Ha. It would serve Nicholas Stoltzfus right. Who didn't like six-year-olds? Her boys were adorable.

The day before, Nicholas had put a gate in the fence line between their property. It helped her *dat* not to have to walk around to the road, and it made sense because the goats would be grazing on both sides. She was a little surprised that he hadn't put up a Twins Keep Out sign as well.

As they hurried through the gate, a pickup truck pulling a trailer turned into the drive. The *Englischer* driving the vehicle backed up to a pen that looked as if it had been hastily put together.

Jacob and Joseph dashed ahead.

Hearing the boys' shouts of delight, Nicholas's head jerked up, and he met her gaze. Deborah was sure he was about to say something, to remind her of the promise to keep the boys on her side of the fence, but then his gaze shifted to her *dat*.

"John."

"Nick. It's *gut* to see you."

Deborah couldn't help shaking her head, remembering her neighbor's insistence that she use his full name. *Nicholas*, he had corrected her with a glare. Good grief. What was this guy's problem?

Still, it was a beautiful day, and the goats were here. She would focus on the fun of the moment.

"Brought my *grandkinner* to help with the goats."

"Oh, well, I don't think…"

"It's the least I can do, and it'll be *gut* for the boys. They're plenty old enough to learn the workings of a farm." Her *dat* waved Jacob and Joseph toward the trailer of goats. "Go on now. Do whatever Nick asks you to do."

The boys looked to Deborah, who echoed, "Yes, do what *Nick* asks you to do."

He looked ready to argue, but then the man driving the truck stepped out, had Nick sign a receipt for the goats and began off-loading them.

Everything was going well, the goats stampeding down the ramp and into the small pen. The problem came when Nick closed the gate, then turned to wave a hand to the *Englischer* as he drove away. The gate must not have fastened, and of course Jacob was perched on it, leaning over the top. His weight caused the gate to swing open.

Jacob let out a "Yee-haw," as if he were a cowboy riding a bull.

Joseph's hands flew to cover his mouth as the goats stampeded toward him. He jumped out of their way and landed on his bottom in the dirt. Blue, who had been smelling the sides of the pen—dashing back and forth as if he could count the new arrivals—didn't even hesitate. He took off after the renegade goats, barking and circling them back toward the gate. Jacob hopped off the fence, waving his hands in an attempt to be helpful.

Unfortunately, that drove the goats back away from the pen.

Nick tried to intervene, as did Deborah. She didn't know what to do, but it couldn't be that much harder than chickens, and she'd dealt with those since she was six. She glanced back and saw her *dat* standing at the pen, ready to close the gate once the goats were back inside.

The goats were various sizes and colors. There were quite a few does and at least half a dozen kids. No billy goats that she could see, which was probably a *gut* thing. But the females must have been frightened and tired, and they also looked very thirsty. They headed straight toward a cattle trough, which was obviously too tall for them. That didn't slow down the lead doe, who proceeded to climb up on top of the pails sitting next to the trough, bleating loudly and calling the other goats toward her.

Blue circled around, barking with great enthusiasm.

The lead goat held her ground.

Blue cut right.

Another large doe cut left and ran into Deborah as she arrived on the scene.

"Oh…" She tried to lean forward, to regain her balance, but it was too late. She plopped into the stock tank, bottom first, with a splash. The water was cold, and the trough wasn't especially clean. She put her hands down, only to slip in slime that had accumulated on the bottom. She came up gasping for air and struggling to pull herself free.

Then two strong arms lifted her up and out and onto solid ground. She looked into Nicholas's eyes, hoping to see laughter there.

Not a chance.

As usual, his lips formed a straight line.

She was dripping wet and more than a little irritated, but as always, her thoughts immediately turned to Jacob and Joseph. They'd frozen in place—Jacob now on top of the pails where the goat had been, Joseph halfway between the pen and the trough. Both boys were silent, waiting, worried.

She could practically read their minds. Was this their fault? Were they in trouble?

And she couldn't stop herself.

Despite her wet clothes, her dripping hair and the look of irritation on Nicholas's face, she started laughing—and once she started, she couldn't stop. She laughed until her sides hurt. The boys joined in, running up next to her.

"You looked like you were swimming, *Mamm*."

"You looked like you were searching for fish."

"Now you won't have to wash your dress."

"Just wring it out and put it on the line."

Taking in her two redheaded boys, smiles on their faces and laughter in their eyes, how could she be angry? This was a story they would tell until she was old and gray. Of course, at this rate, she might become old and gray much sooner than one would expect.

She glanced over at her *dat*, who also had a smile on his face.

And that, too, was worth her own misery. To see the worry fall away from her *dat*'s expression, if only for a moment, she would have slipped in a dozen watering troughs.

Blue, unencumbered by two energetic six-year-olds, had smoothly herded the goats into the pen, and her father slapped the gate shut, tapping down on the crossbar to be sure that it would stay closed.

Nick couldn't imagine a worse start to the Goat Venture. That's how he thought of it now—with capital letters. He'd hoped that the Mast family would head home after Deborah's dunking in the trough, but unfortunately, that didn't happen. John wanted to discuss housing for the goats as well as mineral supplements. He'd apparently done quite a bit of reading on the raising of goats, something that Nick had meant to do but hadn't quite found time for yet.

The boys proceeded to lean on the fence—thankfully not the gate—and call out names for the goats. Molly and Daisy and Ladybug. Buttons and Bobbins for two kids. Rose and Lola. Jethro for a particularly large doe—that name would have to be changed, since it was a female. Who named goats, anyway? Maybe the boys would forget or, better yet, be distracted by the next great thing, which hopefully would not be on his property.

A doe with a lightly tanned coat became Butter.

And the lead goat, the one that had drawn the others over to the water trough, they named Bertha.

Deborah even joined in the game. When the boys couldn't decide on names for the last two, she stood between them—dress drying in the summer sun—and suggested Ginger and Nutmeg.

The boys high-fived, then raced off after their *daddi*, who'd waved goodbye, calling out that he'd be back the next day.

John and his grandsons would be back tomorrow. *Good grief.*

Nick needed to do something before this venture spiraled completely out of control.

He hurried over to speak with Deborah, but she'd turned toward her family. He reached out, snagged her arm, then jumped back when she turned to look at him.

"Sorry."

"For?"

"I'm not sure." He shuffled his feet, stared off at the retreating boys and summoned his courage. "Listen, can we talk for a moment?"

"Sure, Nicholas…" She smiled and leaned a little closer. "Or is it Nick?"

He felt hot around the collar of his shirt and resisted the urge to tug on it. "Nick, actually." He started to add, "My friends call me Nick," but that seemed rather petty, since he'd specifically corrected her when she'd used the shortened version. He swallowed the explanation, ignored her knowing smile and focused on what he wanted to say.

"We didn't get off to a very *gut* start," he began.

"True enough."

"And since we are going to be neighbors—"

"Apparently…"

"I thought it best if I was just honest with you."

"More honest than before? When you told me I should take a stronger hand with my boys?"

"You should. They're out of control."

Her look of surprise quickly changed into exasperation. Closing her eyes, she pulled in a deep breath, probably counted to five, then opened them again and offered a smile—a colder, less sincere smile. "What advice did you want to offer today, Nick?"

"It's not advice so much as…as a plea." He took off his hat, slapped it against his pants leg, then turned back toward the penned goats, who were now huddled on the far side of the enclosure. "Look, you don't know me, and I don't know you. But I came back to Indiana and bought this place because things didn't go well up north. Now all I want is to be left alone, to farm and do my part in the community, and to…"

When he couldn't find the words, she suggested, "Not be bothered?"

"Yes. Exactly." He turned to her now, studied her in her mud-covered dress. As usual, her *kapp* was pushed back, revealing her blond hair. She didn't seem to care about how she appeared or what others thought. Perhaps they had that one thing in common. "I have a five-year plan, and I can't afford to be distracted."

"A five-year plan?" Now she looked at him with undisguised curiosity, as if he'd said something incomprehensible.

"To get this place up and running. Actually, I have one-, three- and five-year plans." He could practically see the neatly written-out business goals, the timeline, the projected costs and income.

Deborah crossed her arms, then pressed her fingers to her lips.

"It's not funny. Why would you think that's funny?"

"Oh, I don't know. Because no one else has such a thing. You don't plan a farm. You work a farm."

"You can still plan."

"Why would you?"

"Why wouldn't I?"

They stood only a foot apart, hands at their sides, scowls on their faces, ready to do battle. Nick took a step back. "Your *dat* seems intent on involving the boys with the goat-raising venture."

"He is. He reminded me on the walk over that I was their age when I was given the chore of caring for our chickens." Now she leaned back against the fence and crossed her arms, staring toward her parents' place, toward her boys. "He's right. It's time they learned responsibility."

"Can't they do that on your place and stay out of my way?"

She sent him a pointed look.

He held up his hands and muttered, "No offense."

"And yet offense is taken." She didn't look peeved, but neither did she back down. "Look, as you pointed out, this was my *dat*'s idea, not mine. I've kept my part of the bargain we made two days ago. I've kept the boys away from you."

"And I appreciate that. It's been a blessedly quiet two days, until…"

"Until what? Your goats had a free run before going in their pen? What is your problem? Why are you so… so stiff?"

"Stiff?"

"Formal."

"I'm formal?"

"You're incorrigible, but I was trying to use small words." Now she laughed.

Her words indicated she'd lost her patience with him, but she laughed.

He did not understand women, and he most certainly did not understand Deborah Mast—nor did he want to. He'd learned his lesson in Maine. He was done with women.

Perhaps he should try a different approach.

"Goats are inexpensive to purchase." He waved the receipt at her. "It seemed like a *gut* idea when your *dat* suggested working together. I'm not ready for all that is involved with caring for a milk cow, but the goats will provide what I need plus some. I should be able to sell the extra milk to a bigger place—"

"Yoder's will take all you can sell them."

"Exactly, but still it's probably not a *gut* idea for your sons to get attached. Goats come and go. Sometimes they have to be sold. Sometimes they die of natural causes..." His words trailed off, sounding pathetic even to his own ears.

"You're worried about Jacob and Joseph? About their feelings?"

"I'm simply pointing out that maybe you'd rather they not be involved."

Deborah took her time straightening her dress, brushing a hand over the mud stains and choosing her words. She stepped closer to him—closer than he was comfortable with, but he wasn't about to back up standing in his own front yard.

"They are involved, though, because you made a deal with my *dat*. If you want out of that deal, speak with him. Now, if you'll excuse me, I have a dress to wash."

He watched her walk away—head held high, *kapp* strings bouncing. He was at a complete loss as to what to do next. Anyone could see that Jacob and Joseph weren't ready to help with goats. Some six-year-olds might be, but those two weren't. They were a menace!

The old cartoon *Dennis the Menace* popped into his mind, but he brushed it away. This was no laughing matter. This was his farm, and he had the right to run it as he saw fit.

If Deborah couldn't see the logic in that, he'd have to

talk to someone else. He didn't want to bother John— the man obviously had enough to deal with just recovering from his stroke. He walked with such a pronounced limp that Nick had noticed it right away.

Which left one person that he could think of.

One person who could and would intercede on his behalf.

One person that Deborah might actually listen to.

He'd speak to the bishop on Sunday.

Chapter Three

Nicholas barely heard a word of the Sunday sermons—either one of them. When he'd arrived at the bishop's house, where Sunday service was being held that week, he'd walked straight to the first open seat he'd seen on the men's side and sat next to his younger *bruder* David. Unfortunately, John Mast took the seat on his left, which meant that Jacob and Joseph crowded in the row as well.

The boys squirmed, giggled, left for a drink of water, returned, then left again for a bathroom visit. The last time, they came back with a suspicious lump in Jacob's coat pocket. At least, Nick thought it was Jacob. The boys were identical in every way—same height, same build, same red hair and freckles. But he was learning that Jacob was the instigator. It made sense, when he thought of the old biblical story of Jacob fighting with the angel. Yes, that name seemed to fit.

Whereas Joseph was quieter, more thoughtful, more like a carpenter, as Jesus's father, Joseph, was.

The lump in Jacob's pocket made an occasional *ribbit* sound. If John Mast noticed, he ignored it.

The man sang with gusto.

Bowed his head during the prayers.

Offered *amens* during the sermons.

He seemed oblivious to what was going on to his left.

Maybe he couldn't see what was going on to his left. Had the stroke affected his vision? Or perhaps the stroke had taught him what was important and what wasn't.

Nicholas pushed that thought away, because it wasn't his problem. His problem was the two boys with their heads bowed, pretending to pray but in fact studying a toad.

When the service was done, Nick made his way to the serving line. Wouldn't you know it, pretty Deborah Mast was helping at the main dish table, wearing a clean pale blue dress and starched white *kapp*. In that moment, he almost let go of whatever animosity had built up between them. But then she said, "*Gut* morning, *Nicholas*."

She wasn't going to allow him to forget their first meeting. That was fine with him, because he hadn't forgotten how much trouble her boys were. Nick was going to talk to the bishop as soon as the meal was over, and perhaps he could put a stop to this situation before it spiraled further out of control.

"Would you like chicken or ham? Or both?"

"Either is fine."

She plopped two large pieces on his plate, then turned to the person behind him. He'd basically been dismissed. He finished filling his plate, then sat beside his *bruder* David, with his wife and three kids crowded in beside them. On the other side of the table sat David's neighbor Silas, with his family. Silas's wife, Freida, had tried to set Nick up with her younger *schweschder*. He'd adamantly refused, and she'd been cool to him since— turning away every time she saw him. Why couldn't people just leave his private life alone?

He focused on eating, attempted to be polite and waited for the bishop to go for a stroll. Bishop Ezekiel always stood and went for a walk after eating. It was basically an open invitation for anyone who would like a private word to approach. Nick fairly catapulted out of his seat when he saw Ezekiel go to the front tables to scrape his plate clean. Before he'd stepped away from the table, Nick was at his side.

"Could I have a word, Bishop?"

"Of course, Nick. Let's walk to the pasture fence and look at the new foal."

Ezekiel's farm wasn't particularly large, but it was well cared for. His youngest son, Paul, had taken over the main job of handling the place. Nick gazed around him in approval. Everything looked to be shipshape. He hoped that by the end of the first year, his place would look the same.

Ezekiel was old for a bishop. Though the job of bishop was for life, many gave additional responsibilities to their deacons as they aged. Ezekiel was at least eighty, and he didn't seem to be slowing down much. His skin was wrinkled, his eyes kind and he used a cane—his only concession to an old knee injury. "A foal is an amazing thing. Don't you think?"

Nick did not want to talk about horses, but he nodded his head in agreement. The foal they were watching was still a bit uncoordinated—its gait changing from slow and careful to fast and speedy in a split second. The mare kept a watchful eye on the foal while she grazed nearby.

"When a foal is born, its legs are eighty to ninety percent of their adult length, and they can stand and walk within two hours of birth." Ezekiel nodded at the black foal with white socks. "Most are born at night, as this one was, and they weigh approximately ten percent of the mother's weight. Nature is amazing. *Gotte* is amazing."

"*Ya.* Indeed." Nick tried to refocus the conversation. "Ezekiel, I was wondering if perhaps I could speak to you about my neighbors."

"The Mast family? *Wunderbaar* people."

"I'm sure, but the thing is that the boys..."

"Are growing at the speed of this colt." The bishop laughed. "I remember when Deborah first had them— two little redheaded bundles. Those boys are a real blessing to Deborah, her parents and our community."

"*Ya.*" The conversation wasn't going the way he wanted it to go at all.

"Have you considered courting Deborah? I think her parents would approve."

"*Nein!*" The word came out more sharply than he intended, and Nick could feel his face blush with embarrassment.

"Deborah is a *gut* woman, a *gut* Christian. You're single and live next door. Sounds like a match made in—"

Nick held up his hand before he could say *heaven.* "I'm not in a place where I'm ready to begin courting."

"Financially?"

"Emotionally."

"Ah." Ezekiel nodded as if he understood what Nick was trying to say.

"What I wanted to speak to you about is Jacob and Joseph. Those two boys are quite the handful..."

"All the more reason for the Mast family to be glad you're next door."

"Oh, I don't think Deborah feels that way at all."

"A neighbor can have a large influence on a child, Nick."

"Yes, but that's not what I'm trying to say."

Ezekiel looked fully at him now, and waited.

"What I'm trying to say is that I'd like you to speak to them—the boys. Or maybe just to Deborah." Sweat trickled down his back. "To the family, I mean."

"About?"

"About respecting boundaries."

"Boundaries?"

"Property lines, fences, another man's property." The words landed like sharp stones on the ground between them.

Ezekiel didn't interrupt. He didn't say anything at all, as if he needed to be sure Nick was done.

Then he smiled, tapped his cane against the ground and began walking toward the play area, where the children had congregated. They didn't speak as they walked, but when they came to the shade of a maple tree, Ezekiel sat at a picnic table, and Nick joined him. They were close enough to the children for their laughter to reach them, but far enough away that they could still easily talk over the noise.

There had to be two or three dozen of them—different sizes and shapes, girls and boys, all full of energy. They tumbled down the slide, chased one another through the green grass, pushed one another on the swings. Jacob, Joseph and several other boys were in the corner of the play area where a birdbath sat, filled with water. Nick could practically see in his mind's eye the toad they were releasing back into nature.

Ezekiel drummed his fingers against the top of his cane. "Do you know what Paul wrote in the fifth chapter of Galatians?"

"Can't say as I do."

"That all of the law can be fulfilled in one word— in one idea, so to speak. Isn't that marvelous?" Ezekiel combed his fingers through his white beard, then raised and lowered his eyebrows. "Think of it, Nick. To follow His way, we don't have to remember a list of rules or follow certain traditions. We don't have to offer specific types of sacrifices on certain days. *Nein*—Paul made it clear that those things are not what make you a true believer."

In spite of himself, Nick was caught up in what the man was saying, what he was describing. He was thinking of his business plan and of Deborah's laughing at him about having such a thing. He was the kind of person who liked a plan, and he did believe they were necessary. But what Ezekiel was saying… Could anything really be that simple? Could anything of real importance be simplified down to a single idea?

"Love thy neighbor as thyself." Ezekiel met his gaze and smiled. "That's it. Easy to remember, *ya*?"

"But maybe not so easy to do."

"You've hit on the very thing I was going to point out—not so easy to do."

"You're saying…" He stopped, unable or unwilling to follow Ezekiel's line of thought.

"I'm saying that you're not merely struggling with the antics of two energetic boys, or even with having neighbors who will—by both proximity and necessity— be involved with your life. And mark my words, your neighbors *will* be involved with your life. You can either embrace that or fight it, but it's the way of the world. No man is an island unto himself."

"Proverb?"

"John Donne—British poet, seventeenth century."

Nick sat forward, elbows on knees, head in his hands. "I take it I haven't been much help."

"Well, you didn't give me the answer I wanted."

"Sleep on it. Pray on it. Your heart will tell you what to do."

But Nick wasn't thinking of his heart. He was thinking of the pages of carefully detailed business plans and how two six-year-old boys could make every single line on those pages more difficult.

Ezekiel was called away by another congregant needing a private word, and Nick was left alone. He watched the children—energetic, happy, growing. He glanced back over his shoulder at the colt that was now galloping about the pasture—awkward still, all legs, growing.

Nick was a farmer. He understood what it took for something to grow into what it should be. A plant needed sun, water, nutrients. A crop was nothing more than a collection of plants. The goats he'd purchased needed the same, but they also needed structure and training. Leave a gate open and a goat could be hurt or injured. Fail to care for them and they could become sick.

Untrimmed hooves would cause a goat to limp.

A lack of iron could cause weak muscles.

Insufficient copper supplements would result in weight loss and a low milk supply.

And Jacob and Joseph? He supposed that their needs were simple, too. It was obvious that Deborah provided for their home and food and clothing, but structure was what they were missing. They had a lot of energy, like his goats, and that energy needed to be funneled.

Nick didn't want the job. It would take time and attention to be done right, and he had other things to do.

But ignoring what needed to be done would result in trouble—double trouble, in this case.

He'd go home, work out a plan and then he'd present it to Deborah. Surely she would see the logic of what he proposed. No, he wasn't an expert on raising children, but he could see things a bit more objectively than she could. Maybe she'd even thank him for offering to help.

Monday afternoon found Deborah outside, beating the living room rug with surprising gusto. She was frustrated, and she fully intended to take it out on the rug. Sunday hadn't been the day of rest that she'd hoped it might be. The fact that she was beginning the week tired and out of sorts irritated her even more.

After they'd arrived home from church, her parents had brought up courting again. Why couldn't they let things be? She was happy—or rather, she was happy enough. Were her boys really suffering from not having a father? They had her *dat*. A man couldn't possibly add anything to her life but additional laundry, unreasonable expectations and heartache.

Holding the broom like a baseball bat, she whopped it against the old rug that she'd draped over the porch railing.

She wanted to enjoy Sundays, to rest, to learn spiritual truths and spend time with her friends.

Whop.

She did not want to have to fend off unwelcome advances from old widowers.

Whop. Whop.

And she did not want to even think about what Nick had said to Bishop Ezekiel. He'd definitely looked over his shoulder at her as they'd walked away.

Another solid whop.

Dust rose from the old rug, and she peered through it. Nick Stoltzfus was making his daily trip to speak to her *dat*. He was early. Usually he waited until she was inside cooking.

Blue walked by his side, which was an instant attraction for her boys. They surrounded Nick and the dog, laughing and waving their arms back and forth, explaining something that Nick was obviously not listening to. His eyes were locked on hers. She knew that look. He was coming back for round two, or was it three?

Instead of putting up the broom, she whacked the rug again, but this time with less focus. Barely any dust rose at all. Nick looked as if he was about to give her advice on how to clean a rug. Fortunately for him, Jacob interrupted whatever he might have said.

"I have a ball in the backyard...an old tennis ball. Do you think Blue would chase that?"

"I suspect he would." Nick never looked away from her, so Deborah set down the broom and crossed her arms.

Best to get this over with.

Jacob ran to fetch the ball for the dog.

Joseph dropped to his knees and proceeded to lavish affection on the blue heeler—rubbing his belly and stroking his ears.

Nick stepped closer to the porch. "Can I speak with you?"

"Of course."

But then he didn't seem to know how to proceed, which struck Deborah as funny. The one thing she knew about the man standing in front of her was that he had no problem speaking his mind. So why the hesitation?

Nick sank onto the front porch step, as if he no longer had the energy to continue standing. Deborah was not falling for that. She refused to feel sympathy for Nicholas Stoltzfus.

On the other hand, she was tired from a long day of cleaning house. She sank down on the step next to him.

"I spoke with Bishop Ezekiel yesterday."

"*Ya*, I saw you two walking off together."

"To be honest..."

Deborah felt herself tense.

"I was wanting him to resolve...this." He waved at the boys.

"Resolve?"

"Clear up our differences, make a useful suggestion, determine our next step." Nick rubbed his hands over his face. "Honestly, I don't know what I expected him to do."

He glanced her way, and Deborah saw that the exhaustion lines around his eyes matched her own. What was keeping him up nights? Problems with his five-year plan?

"I wasn't expecting *this*, Deborah. I wasn't prepared."

"What is *this*?"

Instead of answering, he pushed on. "I thought I could buy a little place and make up for the Lost Years in Maine—that's how I think of them, like a book title with capital letters. But it's not working out as simply as I had hoped."

"And that's Jacob's fault? That's Joseph's doing?"

"I never said either of those things." He gave her a sideways look. "You're quite defensive when it comes to your boys."

"Comes with the job description."

"You remind me of a mama bear."

"And you've met one of those?"

He laughed, though it came out sounding more like a bark. "*Nein*, but I can imagine one well enough."

Jacob had returned from the backyard. He tossed the ball in the air, and Blue went scurrying after it, retrieved it and returned it to Jacob.

"I want to try." Joseph repeated the throw, with the same result.

The boys were beside themselves with amazement.

"Did you see that?"

"Did you see Blue?"

"He's so smart."

"Smarter than a circus dog."

They continued playing with Blue, and Deborah braced herself for whatever Nick was about to throw at her. She guessed she wouldn't like it, but suddenly she was too tired to fight. Perhaps she was sick. Maybe she was catching a cold. Or possibly raising twin boys took more energy than she had some days.

"I'd like to help you raise the boys."

Deborah almost fell off the step. She opened her mouth to speak, but nothing came out. What could she even say? How was she supposed to respond to such a completely unexpected and ludicrous suggestion?

"It can't be easy, doing it alone. Also, it's plain that your *dat* has his hands full with this place and his health concerns."

"You want to help *raise* Jacob and Joseph?"

The shock in her voice must have surprised him, because he turned to look at her quizzically.

"What? Why are you looking at me that way?" He rubbed the back of his neck, glanced at her again, then clasped his hands together.

And then the laughter did win, spilling out of her like water from a faucet. The boys turned to look at her, shrugged their small shoulders and resumed running back and forth with the dog. Nick shook his head as if she made no sense at all—as if she was the one who had said something incomprehensible.

Nick cleared his throat. "I don't mean to be too familiar, but we are neighbors, as the bishop pointed out. We have a duty to one another as members of the same church community, and—" He took off his hat, reshaped it with his fingers, then plopped it back on his head.

He wasn't a bad-looking man. It was just that he so rarely smiled. What had happened to give him such a sour disposition? Or was he born with it? She'd had an *aenti* who could point out the flaw in any handmade quilt, knitted shawl or baked cake. She wasn't even aware when she did it. She seemed to have no idea why the rest of the family avoided being alone with her.

But Nick knew what he was doing, because a blush was creeping up his neck. He was embarrassed but not backing down. He honestly thought he could do a better job of raising her own sons than she could. The arrogance of the man amazed her.

And yet, she was curious.

Or perhaps she simply wanted the satisfaction of hearing him concede he was wrong—which she suspected wouldn't take very long. A week? A day? Possibly even a couple of hours, and then he'd be apologizing and admitting that he had grossly underestimated how much time and energy and wisdom it took to raise two boys.

She patted her cheeks to cool them, then cleared her throat. "You're making a couple of assumptions that I probably don't agree with."

"Such as?"

"You think I need help."

"Don't you?"

"Some days I could use a hand—I'll admit that. But I'm not sure you're it." When he looked at her in surprise, she added, "It's not as if you've had a lot of experience. You've not been married and have no children of your own."

"I've never raised goats before, either, but they're doing quite well."

"Children are not goats."

"I didn't say they were, but honestly…can it be that much harder?"

This time Deborah literally prayed for patience before answering. "What exactly did you have in mind?"

"I was thinking that they could come over for an hour in the morning…" He swallowed visibly, as if the words were difficult to spit out. "And an hour in the afternoon. I'll show them how to properly care for the goats, maybe a few other everyday chores."

"So basically, you want my boys to be your farm hands, for free."

Nick pulled at his left ear, now refusing to meet her gaze. "It's not as if I expect them to be that much help. Why would I pay them? Perhaps we could think of it more as a free apprenticeship."

"They are six years old." She emphasized the last three words, because she still didn't think he understood that they were *kinner*. They weren't *youngies* looking for their life work. They were boys waiting for the school term to begin. "They turn seven in July and start school in the fall."

"Great. Only a few months, then." Nick grinned, then schooled his expression. He must have realized that he sounded overly relieved to know his apprentices wouldn't be around forever. "Sorry. What I meant to say is that for the summer, I think it could be a *gut* arrangement, and then during the school year I expect they'll be too busy."

She didn't answer. She didn't know what to say.

"And the things they learn at my place, they'll be able to use here…to help your *dat*."

Why did he have to add that particular point? If there was one chink in her motherly armor, it was that she felt guilty for piling more work on her parents' plate. If the boys could learn to be helpful rather than exhausting…well, she supposed it might be worth considering Nick's idea.

"You won't have them do anything too difficult?"

"Of course not."

"I wouldn't want them to get hurt."

"And I wouldn't let that happen."

She stood, walked down the steps of the porch and stared at her sons. They had a lot of energy. Truthfully, she wouldn't mind having a couple of hours free of her parenting responsibilities, though she'd probably spend the time beating rugs and gardening. What else did she have to do? The boys were her life. They were what she planned her day around. She could no longer remember who she'd been or what she'd done before having them. Surely she'd had hobbies and interests.

She'd forgotten all about those things, left them behind when she'd picked up her first diaper. There'd been no point—no time. It seemed she rarely had even a moment for herself anymore. She'd almost forgotten what it felt like.

"Okay. We'll give it a try."

Nick actually smiled. "You won't be sorry."

"But you might. Twins aren't as easy as you apparently think."

"Oh, that. Well, I have four *bruders* and three *schweschdern*, all younger than I am."

So, he was the oldest. Somehow that wasn't a surprise. The oldest sibling tended to be the bossiest—at least that was true in Deborah's family, and her oldest *schweschder*, Molly, would readily admit to it.

"Twins can't be harder than seven younger siblings," he added. He was once again confident.

It made her want to roll her eyes or laugh or shake him good and hard. She glanced toward the house in time to see her *mamm* peeking out the window. She actually gave Deborah a thumbs-up sign, then darted out of sight.

"What just happened?" Nick turned to look behind him, then faced her again. "You were all for it, and now I can see you're hesitating."

"*Nein*. It's just—I have a problem of my own." She studied him, then added, "A problem you might be able to help me with."

"I'm already helping you with the boys."

"Uh-uh. That's me doing you a favor, though I won't pretend to understand why you came up with this idea to begin with. Still, maybe we can help each other."

"What do you need help with?"

She pulled in her bottom lip. Was she actually going to suggest this? Then the curtain over the kitchen window moved again, and she knew she was going to have to do something soon or her *mamm* would have all the eligible men in the county lining up down the lane. That list! She did not want to think about it. Instead, she tugged on Nick's arm and pulled him away from the front porch, out of the hearing of her well-intentioned *mamm*.

"My parents want me to begin courting."

"I'm not interested." Nick's ears turned a rosy red when she stared at him. "Not that you're not..."

"What?"

"I just mean that you're nice-looking enough."

"Compliments like that will surely go straight to my head."

"I'm not interested in courting in general, is what I mean. I want to focus on my—"

"Five-year plan. I'm aware. Here's the thing, Nick. I'm not interested, either, but my *mamm* is pretty determined. She's not going to back down unless she thinks that I'm courting."

"Oh."

"It doesn't have to be real."

"'Course not."

"I'm no more interested in you than you are in me."

He looked slightly offended, but she pushed on. "My boys will apprentice with you, for free, and in return you and I pretend to court."

"For how long?"

She tapped a finger against her lips. Yes, she could do this. Her *mamm* volunteered at the school in the fall, so she'd be too busy to worry about matchmaking. "Through the summer. That should calm my parents down a bit. At the end of the summer, we'll make up some excuse as to why it wouldn't work."

"That shouldn't be hard, since we're complete opposites."

"I noticed." She smiled up at him, then held out her hand. "Deal?"

"What is it with you people and shaking hands? It's a very *Englisch* thing to do."

"Is it a deal or not?"

"Ya." He shook and mumbled, "I suppose."

"Gut." They walked back toward the porch. "Now about the boys…"

"They can start tomorrow."

"Why not now?"

"What?" He'd been looking quite pleased with himself, but that look vanished. "Now…today now? Bad idea. I'm not ready."

"Not ready?"

"I was going to make some lists—of daily chores. Maybe tack it above a cubby in the barn, where the boys can keep their tools and check off each item."

"They're *gut* readers for their age, but I'm not sure that will work. Remember, they're six."

"Have you tried it?"

"Nein. I talk to them. I don't have to leave them a note."

Nick's eyes darted to the boys and back to her. "I mean, I'll tack it there and we'll see how it works. But I'll follow up—verbally."

Deborah only wished she could be a fly on the wall in that barn when he set this plan into motion.

Nick looked across the yard and called Blue to his side. The boys followed as if they were invisibly tied to the dog.

"Jacob and Joseph, I have some *gut* news for you." Deborah nodded toward their neighbor. "Nick has offered to teach you how to raise goats."

The boys' eyes widened in surprise, then they high-fived one another and attempted to high-five Nick, who simply looked at them as if he didn't know what they wanted.

"You'll spend an hour at his place in the morning and an hour in the afternoon."

"We could spend all day," Jacob offered.

"*Ya*, there's nothing to do around here. All day would work for me." Joseph glanced at Deborah, suddenly worried about her feelings. "Not that we don't like being here around you. It's just…"

"We'd enjoy doing some guy stuff." Jacob clapped his *bruder* on the back.

"Exactly."

Nick was now standing behind the boys, making very obvious *no* gestures to the idea of all-day helpers.

"Let's start with the two hours and see how that goes. Now fetch the rug that's on the railing and carry it back inside for me, then see if your *mammi* needs any help with dinner."

They ran up the porch steps with the same enthusiasm they'd shown with the dog, struggled to pull the rug off the porch railing and managed to knock over two pots of flowers as they dragged it into the house.

Deborah righted the pots, swept off the dirt and looked up—surprised to see that Nick was still standing there.

"Having second thoughts?"

"*Nein.* Of course not."

"Then the boys will see you tomorrow—9:00 a.m."

"Perfect."

"And we can go on our first…date on Saturday. If that works for you."

"I guess."

She leaned forward and whispered, "I won't expect you to buy me dinner. We can go Dutch."

He nodded, looking as if he wanted to say something else, as if he had more questions or possibly more words of wisdom to impart, but he wisely kept them to himself.

Deborah stood there, watching him walk back across the field to his place. After a moment, she realized that he hadn't spoken with her *dat*. Was he that distracted at the thought of teaching her boys? Then why had he offered?

Or did the thought of dating make him so uncomfortable that he had to tuck tail and run home?

She almost laughed out loud. She'd found the one person who wanted to date less than she did, and she'd coerced him into a fake relationship. Well, he deserved it. And by the end of the summer, she suspected he would have his eye on someone more his type.

In truth, she didn't understand men at all.

Nick spoke with her *dat* every day, updating him on the shelters he was building and how the goats were doing. They were partners, in the full sense of the word—except Nick provided the manpower and her *dat* provided the funds.

Only now her boys would provide part of the manpower.

It gave her a funny feeling, the same mild nausea as when she thought of them attending school. She wanted to see them have these firsts, for them to grow independent and confident. But each step they took was a step away from her, and they were her only children. It was very doubtful she'd marry again and have more. She didn't see that happening.

How could she be sure that a prospective husband would care for her boys as much as she did? How could she trust someone with such a precious part of her life, even more precious than her own heart? Because she could guard her heart. She could stand up for herself if someone was unkind. Her boys were still young, still vulnerable.

Nein. She wouldn't be remarrying anytime soon, or seriously dating, for that matter.

She didn't need to.

She was perfectly happy with her life exactly as it was. Only as she walked into the house, she knew that wasn't precisely true. One part of her was happy enough, but another part was still a young girl expecting to have her own special happily-ever-after.

Chapter Four

He noticed that Deborah had walked over with the boys and was standing by the fence, her hand shielding her eyes from the morning sun. Why did she feel she had to accompany them? The boys knew the way to his place. She really did coddle them, but then Nick supposed that was normal with first-time parents.

She spotted him and waved. He did the same, and she turned and headed back toward her place. She didn't seem any more keen on his plan than she had the day before. He wondered if she'd take to their fake dating with the same lack of enthusiasm. Why had he agreed to that?

He shook the thought from his head, then greeted the boys, who had broken into a trot as soon as they saw Blue.

"Gudemariye."

"Morning, Nick," they replied in unison, somewhat out of breath from their jog.

"We're here to work," one said.

"We waited until nine, like you told us," said the other. "But we could come much earlier."

"I need to know how to tell you apart," he admitted.

When they were getting in trouble, he knew it was Jacob leading the charge. But when they were standing there patiently, red hair neatly combed, hats pushed back and smiles on their faces, he hadn't the slightest idea which was Jacob and which was Joseph. "Any clues?"

The boys laughed, and then Jacob pointed to his left eyebrow. "I have a scar, from the time that we tried to ride one of the old buggy wheels down the hill."

"Didn't work," Joseph explained. "He crashed."

"Got it. *Danki.*"

"Gem gschehne," they again replied in unison.

"So, do you want us to come earlier?" Jacob asked.

"Nine is fine. I have other things to do before you get here."

"Oh. Maybe we could help with those things."

"Let's see how you do with the goats before we add to your chores."

"Got it," Jacob said.

"Let me show you where your cubby is."

"We have a cubby?" Joseph's voice rose a notch.

The boys shared an incredulous look, then high-fived one another. They had plenty of enthusiasm, that was for certain.

He took them to the barn and showed them the cubbies he had designated for their use.

"They have our names." Joseph traced the letters.

Jacob hopped from one foot to another. "And it's in permanent marker."

Nick realized he hadn't quite thought that through, but a permanent marker was all that had been handy. Did he consider the boys as permanent farm hands? He did not. Still, the permanent ink was a minor problem for another day.

He had explained to them that they were responsible

for returning their tools at the end of their work time. "Your chore list will be here every day. I want you to check it, first thing."

"Only has one item on it." Joseph squinted at the sheet of paper in puzzlement.

"'Build goat playground.'" Jacob took off his hat and tossed it in the air, missed catching it, lurched forward, crashed to the ground and landed on top of the hat. "This is going to be awesome."

"I'll give you a longer list when I'm sure you can properly finish one thing, and we'll need to get you some work gloves."

"*Daddi* sent some." Joseph pulled his gloves from his back pocket, as did Jacob.

Jacob frowned at the single glove in his hand. "I had two when I left the house."

"Trace your way back and find the other, then meet Joseph and me in the goat pen." Jacob was almost to the barn door when Nick called him back. "Don't let any of the goats out when you come into the pen. And maybe... walk instead of run, so that you don't frighten them."

"*Gut* idea." Jacob flashed a smile and took off at a run.

Blue looked confused as to whether he should follow Jacob or stay with Joseph. Perhaps his dog needed the energy of young boys, because Nick seemed to have lost the mutt's allegiance in a very short amount of time. Plainly the dog preferred the boys' company to his. Well, what dog wouldn't? Nick rarely took the time to toss a ball or give the mutt a tummy rub.

"With us, Blue."

Nick planned to spend the next hour introducing the boys to the goats and showing them what he wanted them to build. He didn't expect them to accomplish much, but perhaps they could start building the structure when they came back in the afternoon.

Things didn't go exactly as he'd planned.

Jacob returned, taking giant, deliberate steps as if he was playing a game of Mother May I. The goats immediately ran to the opposite side of the pen.

"Why are you walking that way?"

Jacob froze midstride. "Because you told me not to run."

"Just walk, normal like."

"Oh." He cocked his head, raised a foot, then set it back down. "I normally run."

"Hurry up, will you?" Joseph sounded as impatient as Nick felt. "I mean, hurry up, but slowly. Nick was just about to tell us some interesting goat stuff."

"It's important that you learn to use the correct words. A female goat is a nanny or a doe."

"What about the males?" Jacob peered under the closest goat, trying to get a closer look.

"We don't have any males, but if we did, they would be called a billy or a buck."

"Why don't we have any males?" Joseph asked.

"Because we don't want any pregnant does yet."

Jacob scratched his head. "I don't really understand how that happens."

"Ask your *daddi* or your *mamm*." Nick did not plan on explaining the birds and the bees to these two. "Younger goats are called kids."

Which sent the boys into peals of laughter.

"And remember, a bored goat is a problem goat."

"Same thing *Mamm* says about us," Joseph noted.

"I've brought over some old tires and crates, and there's a cluster of rocks over there. Today, your job is to—"

"Build a goat playground. Just like it said on our chore list." Joseph looked up with a smile, as if he was expecting a gold star.

"Right. First of all, stack the tires and crates around the rocks so that it resembles a climbing area. You want it to be nice and solid—no wobbly crates. As you work, let the goats get comfortable around you. No running or shouting. That stirs them up."

Jacob had been about to shout. Now he buttoned his lips closed.

"What are you going to do?" Joseph asked.

He'd planned on staying in the goat pen with them, but how hard could it be to stack up crates and tires? They needed to learn how to work without supervision. Now was as good a time as any to see how they'd do.

"I'll be in that field, checking the crop." He pointed to the west. "Do you both know how to whistle?"

In response, both boys stuck their fingers in their mouths. Jacob emitted an earsplitting whistle. Joseph pulled his fingers out and stared at them, as if the problem could be found there.

"*Gut*. Do that if you need me, but only if you need me. No fooling around. Taking care of goats—and crops—is serious work."

Both boys attempted grave expressions and stuck their hands in their pockets. Nick had never spent much time around twins. It was amazing how much their mannerisms mirrored one another, and yet in so many ways they seemed to be polar opposites.

Jacob and Joseph assured him that they understood what he wanted them to do.

Nick told Blue to stay, then walked out of the pen, securely fastened the gate and headed toward the west field. He'd planted corn three weeks before. He was happy to see it was coming in nicely. He spent the next thirty minutes walking up and down the rows. It was a perfect June morning—the day had started off cool and was already growing warmer. The sun shone brightly, and a slight breeze stirred from the east.

Things were going well. He congratulated himself on having an organized, well-planned morning. Having defined steps toward his goal always helped to ease his worries. He'd spent two hours the night before reworking the plan for his farm, for his life. The boys wouldn't really slow anything down, not if he could teach them to be *gut* workers.

Twins weren't so difficult.

No doubt, Deborah was a good *mamm.* He suspected she simply wasn't methodical enough. Often people didn't realize how important it was to think through a thing. Maybe he would be a good influence on her. Stranger things had happened. As for their dating—he rather wished he hadn't agreed to that, but backing out now didn't feel right, either.

He was puzzling over that and walking toward the far end of the field when he heard someone running and shouting. He turned to see Joseph racing toward him, arms waving, looking as if something was on fire.

"What's wrong?"

"It's Jacob." He bent over, hands on knees. "He fell, and he's…"

He took in another gulp of air, then finished with the last word Nick wanted to hear. "…bleeding."

Deborah pulled two cherry Popsicles out of the freezer and handed them to both boys.

"Danki, Mamm." Joseph smiled up at her as she ruffled his hair. "But I didn't even lose a tooth."

Jacob mumbled something unintelligible as he tried to hold the cold rag to his mouth and stick the Popsicle in at the same time.

"You're both *gut* boys. Now take those out back to the swing set."

Her parents had gone to town for her *dat*'s monthly checkup at the doctor, and Nick was sitting on the front porch—his head in his hands.

She poured him a glass of iced tea, grabbed the container of peanut butter bars and pushed through the front door. "Drink this. It'll help."

He took the tea and downed it in one swallow, but waved away the peanut butter bars. "I have to say...that looked like a lot of blood to me."

Deborah laughed. "Jacob has always been a bleeder when he loses teeth. It doesn't last long."

"And the bump on his head?"

"The swelling is already going down."

He finally looked up and met her gaze. "Took a year off my life at least."

"You get used to it."

"I don't want to get used to it, and I don't understand what happened. Or how it happened so quickly. Or why I didn't anticipate that it might happen."

"You can't plan for everything." Deborah didn't feel nearly as upset as Nick appeared to be. If she panicked every time there was a bruise or scratch or lost tooth, she'd spend a lot of time in a state of fright.

She had only been mildly alarmed to see him hurrying toward the front porch with the boys. She'd rather suspected he'd had his fill of them and was there to *return them to sender*. Nick had arrived at the front porch looking quite shaken and out of breath. One look at the spots of blood on Jacob's shirt and his grin revealing a nice gap between his teeth, and she'd figured out what had happened. She'd whisked them inside.

"I left them there alone. Was that the wrong thing to do?"

"They won't be very *gut* helpers if you have to watch over their shoulders every moment."

Nick nodded as if that made sense. "They understood what I wanted them to do. Why would Jacob decide to climb on top of the stacked crates and jump?" He glanced up at her with a look of such puzzlement that she took mercy on him.

"He's six. That's what I've been trying to tell you. Six-year-olds do things that don't make sense to you or me." She scooted back in her seat and pushed the chair into a gentle rocking rhythm. "When he was only four, he came in crying because he'd climbed to the top of the swing set and jumped off. I asked him why he'd do such a thing, and do you know what he told me?"

"I have no idea." Nick reached for the container of peanut butter bars, selected one and ate it in two bites.

"He told me that it didn't hurt the first time he jumped and only hurt a little the second time, but the third time he was pretty sure he broke something."

Nick shook his head in amazement.

"Turned out it was just a sprain, but who knows why he thought he could do such a thing. Joseph apparently stayed on the ground, marking his distance with a stick in the dirt each time."

"Maybe I should supervise them more closely. Wouldn't want him to knock out all his front teeth."

"I thought you said they did a *gut* job."

"Yeah. They stacked everything so that it's solid and steady. The goats are very happy."

"Then we'll consider today a success."

"But the tooth…"

"Was going to come out anyway. Joseph's shouldn't be far behind."

Nick pulled in a deep breath, then stood. "Well, I'm behind my day's schedule, so I should go. *Danki* for the tea and snack."

"Thank you for walking the boys back."

"Couldn't very well send them home alone, bleeding." He snapped his fingers. "Which reminds me, though, you don't have to walk them over every morning. Plainly, they know the way. Seems a bit…overprotective."

She resisted the urge to sigh. "Maybe I enjoy taking a stroll in the morning."

"Or maybe you're afraid to let them walk from your place to mine alone."

That stung. She wasn't exactly afraid, though she was cautious about letting them out of her sight for too long. Still, she didn't think it was his place to point that out.

"It certainly didn't take you long to fall back into lecture mode."

"I'm not lecturing."

"If you say so."

"Just…a suggestion." He shrugged and walked down the porch steps. Turning and walking backward, he said, "I guess the boys will want the afternoon off."

"Oh, no. They'll be over at four o'clock sharp."

Was that disappointment on his face? Well, this entire plan had been his idea. She wasn't about to let him squirm out of it on the first day, especially because of a little mishap like a tooth popping out.

Nick nodded, as if he'd expected as much. She watched him as he walked toward his place. One minute he could be so normal, and the next he fell into a parental role, or worse than that a big *bruder* role. She didn't need a big *bruder*. She had two older *bruders* and two older *schweschdern*. She'd been bossed around her entire life, but she wasn't going to be bossed around by her neighbor. She drew the line there.

That evening, she sat knitting while her *mamm* worked on the binding of a baby quilt. The boys had gone to bed without any argument, probably owing to the fact that they were worn out. They'd spent their afternoon at Nick's brushing goats. Apparently, that took more energy than one would think, since they spent much of the time chasing the goat that was to be brushed.

Her *dat* had also retired early.

"What did the doctor say?"

"That your *dat* is doing *gut*. That it will take time before he regains the ground he lost with the stroke."

"But he will?"

"There's every reason to believe so." Bethany glanced up and smiled, then added, "*Gotte* willing."

"How could *Gotte* not be willing?" Deborah considered herself to be a person of faith, but that didn't mean that she understood why things happened. Maybe no one did.

"*Gotte*'s ways are not our ways—Isaiah 55, if I remember correctly."

"I guess." Deborah was too tired for a religious discussion. Perhaps she should have rested while the boys were working at Nick's, but instead she'd decided to scrub the oven. What had possessed her to do that?

Unfortunately, her *mamm* wasn't as willing to drop the discussion.

"Your *dat* and I won't live forever. I'm sure you realize that."

"But he's getting better, and you're—you're fine. Aren't you?"

Her *mamm* paused in her sewing and waited for Deborah to meet her gaze. "I'm fine."

"Gut."

"But, Deborah, we must all prepare for the future as best we can."

"Okay."

"It's one of the reasons we want you to date. We won't always be here for you and Jacob and Joseph. It hurts my heart to think about you raising those boys alone."

Every conversation seemed to circle back to this. Deborah wanted to groan in frustration, but instead, she tried reasoning with her *mamm.* "I have four siblings, and they all live relatively close."

Her *bruder* Simon and his family lived down the road. Her older *schweschder* Belinda lived on the far side of Shipshewana with her husband and six *kinner.* Stephen lived in Elkhart with his family, which required hiring an *Englisch* driver to visit. Molly lived in Goshen, which was also too far for a buggy ride. They were all somewhat scattered across northern Indiana, but they didn't live far. It wasn't as if she would be left alone when her parents passed.

"Simon has put an offer on a farm in Middlebury."

"What? Mary didn't tell me that."

"I spoke with them at church."

"And you're just telling me now?"

"It's only an offer. The owners might have received a better offer. It's nothing to get excited about."

"I'm not excited." Why did everything have to change? Why couldn't the world just slow down for a moment?

"Middlebury isn't so far from us, but my point is the same—we want you to have some stability. Yes, your *bruders* and *schweschdern* will always be there for you, but, sweetheart, I'm not just talking financially or practically. I'm talking emotionally, too."

"I think you worry too much." Seeing that her *mamm* wasn't going to let the topic drop, she added, "I forgot to tell you that I have a date for this weekend."

Her *mamm* let out a yelp, dropped the quilt she was working on and stuck her finger in her mouth.

"You don't have to be that surprised."

"Who says I'm surprised?"

"Your eyebrows say you're surprised."

"Who are you going out with? Simon Lapp?"

Ugh. Widower Lapp was twenty years older than her and had six children. Plus, he had a very unkempt beard. How could she look at that every morning? She'd constantly be reminding him to comb it or pluck the food out of it.

"Nick."

"Nick…" Her *mamm* stared up at the ceiling.

"Nick Stoltzfus. Our neighbor!"

"Oh." Her *mamm* plucked a tissue from the box on the coffee table and spent an inordinate amount of time wrapping it around her finger.

"What?"

"Nothing."

"I thought you'd be happy."

"Oh, I am. Of course. *Wunderbaar* news."

"But…"

"It's just that I thought the two of you were at crosswinds with one another."

"What's that supposed to mean?"

"I've never heard you say anything complimentary about him."

"That's not true."

"You said he's bossy."

"He is."

"And that he pretends to know how to raise children when he's never had any."

"Also true."

"And didn't you tell me that he talked to the bishop about the boys?"

"We've worked all that out, *Mamm*. And we're going on a date Saturday evening. I was hoping you could… you know…babysit the boys for me."

"You don't have to ask me to babysit. They're my *grandkinner*, and they live here."

"I'll take that as a yes. *Danki*."

"Your *dat* will be so happy to hear this." Her *mamm* smiled.

"It's just a date, *Mamm*."

"Now it is, but it could turn into more."

"I suppose." Deborah gathered up her knitting. "Today wore me out. I think I'll head to bed early."

"Parenting can be an exhausting thing."

Deborah was afraid her *mamm* would add something to that statement. Like *that's why you need a husband.* Fortunately, she didn't.

Instead, she raised her face when Deborah stopped by her chair, so that Deborah leaned down and kissed her on the cheek. She wasn't quite sure when she'd started doing that, but now it felt as natural and normal as brushing her hair in the morning. Kissing her *mamm*'s weathered cheek reminded her of how very important this woman was to her.

"We love you, Deborah. You're a *gut* girl—a *gut mamm* and a *gut doschder.*"

Deborah nodded and hurried from the room, tears stinging her eyes. For some reason those words pricked her heart more than any criticism could have.

As she readied for bed, she tried to push the conversation with her mother from her mind. Yes, she understood that her parents would not live forever, but they were only in their late fifties. Many people in their community often lived to their eighties. She knew she shouldn't count on that, but there was also no reason to borrow trouble.

She punched her pillow and rolled onto her side.

Simon and Mary were moving?

Middlebury wasn't far, but they would definitely see each other less. Deborah was closer to Simon than any of her siblings. And Mary was like her best friend. Why hadn't they told her? Probably they didn't want to worry her until it was a sure thing.

Was everyone concerned about worrying her?

Did they consider her so very fragile?

She sat up, fluffed the pillow and tried lying on her other side. Sleep continued to elude her. She felt more wide-awake than she had downstairs. Probably she should get up and do some knitting. She didn't, though. Instead, she stared out the window at the night sky, wondering why things always had to change and why she always felt like the one being left behind.

Chapter Five

Deborah stood in front of the pegs where she kept her five dresses, trying to decide which one to wear. *Englischers* were sometimes surprised that they didn't have closets, but who needed one? The pegs and shelf located across from her bed worked fine. She reached out for the church dress, but Mary stopped her.

"Too formal."

"None of my dresses are formal."

"You know what I mean. It screams *church*." Mary was three years older than Deborah. She was tall and thin and one of the nicest people that Deborah knew.

"In case you haven't noticed, all of our clothes look the same."

"The style, yes. But the color, no. The dark blue screams church. The lavender whispers fun."

Deborah turned to give her sister-in-law a pointed look, but Mary didn't back down. "The lavender one looks nice on you. Try it."

"Honestly, I'm a little afraid it won't fit." She pulled the dress over her head. The waistline was snug, but not too tight.

"Very flattering. You have a *gut* figure, Deborah."

"I have a *mamm*'s figure."

"Nothing wrong with that." They shared a smile. Mary had wed Deborah's *bruder* Simon nine years ago. Sadly, they'd only been able to have one child. Christopher was a year older than Deborah's twins, and the younger boys idolized him.

"Are you sure you don't mind taking the boys home with you?"

"I know you're kidding. Christopher has been asking for weeks—since school let out in May."

Deborah had been staring into the mirror as she combed out her hair in order to rebraid it. She met Mary's eyes in the mirror. "I'm going to miss you."

"Middlebury is only eight miles away."

"But it won't be the same."

Mary stood and walked behind her. Taking the comb, she ran it through the back of Deborah's hair. "It reaches past your waist now."

"Remember when the boys hid chewing gum in my chair and I sat back and got it stuck in my hair?"

"Had to cut a *gut* three inches off. You've grown that back and more." Mary finished the braid, twisted it into a bun and secured it with a few hairpins. "Life is always changing, *ya*?"

"I suppose." Deborah picked up her freshly laundered *kapp*, pinned it in place and tried not to frown at her image. She looked older. When had that happened? She plopped down on the bed next to Mary.

"You're no longer the young woman who came home from Ohio all tears and worries. It was snowing and cold when you came to the house and told Simon and me that you were pregnant."

"I was scared and more than a little embarrassed."

"We cried together."

"I had no idea what to do."

"And then we prayed."

Deborah ran a finger across the stitching of her quilt—a friendship quilt that Mary had hand-sewn and given to her. "You and Simon even came over for support when I told *Mamm* and *Dat*."

"We've been through much together."

"It's been a *gut* seven years. I feel safe and protected here. I feel as if the world can't get in. Do you know what I mean?"

Mary nodded and reached for her hands. "But even Plain families have their challenges and troubles, as we both know. Life is always changing, Deborah—even for Plain folk, and I've heard we really like for things to stay the same."

"I wouldn't change what happened to me for anything in the world. I was frightened and worried, and coming back to Shipshe—coming back to our family and our church—was difficult. I didn't want to admit to the mistakes I'd made, and yet doing so opened up a whole new path for me."

"Coming home was the right thing to do."

"As for Jacob and Joseph—they're my heart walking around in work pants, button-up shirts, suspenders and straw hats." Deborah smiled at that, then sobered. "I know what you're thinking, but we won't grow apart."

"We won't?"

"I won't allow it." Mary stood and pulled Deborah to her feet. "Now, do we need to go over the rules of dating?"

"I think I got it."

"It's okay to mention the boys, but don't talk about them all night."

"What else do I have to talk about?"

"Don't pick a fight, either."

"Why would I do that?"

"Find something to compliment him on."

"Nick is confident enough. He doesn't need my compliments to make him feel better."

Mary cocked her head to the side. "I think you intimidate him."

"What?" It came out as a squeal. Deborah fought to lower her voice and asked again, "What?"

"You're intimidating."

"I am not."

"You're an independent woman, a *gut mamm*, and you know your own mind. Plus, you're not afraid to voice your opinions."

"Those things don't make me intimidating."

"They might." Mary stepped forward and embraced Deborah in a hug, then she whispered, "Just have fun."

"It's not even a real date."

"So you've mentioned."

"I'm having second thoughts."

"Too late, because I believe Nick just drove up."

They both moved to the window and looked down. Nick exited the buggy at the same moment Jacob, Joseph and Christopher came running around the corner of the house. Deborah and Mary couldn't make out what was being said, but the boys laughed, high-fived Nick, then ran off.

"He's *gut* with the boys."

"Maybe." They locked gazes once more, then both hurried downstairs and out the front door. Deborah was mortally embarrassed to find her parents on the front porch, as if they needed to check out her date before they were allowed to leave.

Nick looked up, saw her and did a double take. He raised his eyes to hers and smiled appreciatively. Deborah could have easily melted into the porch floor. This wasn't a real date! Surely he remembered that.

The boys returned with something in their hands, making a big show of needing to talk to Nick in private. He turned his back, and apparently items were exchanged. A quarter for each of the boys, if she wasn't mistaken. When Nick turned to face her, he was holding a bouquet of wildflowers.

"Every woman deserves flowers, right?"

"So nice of you to…bring them?"

The boys shouted, "We picked them."

"I never would have guessed."

"My *dat* gives my *mamm* flowers sometimes," Christopher piped up. "And then they kiss."

Jacob made kissing noises, and Joseph shook his head as if to dislodge the thought. Deborah could hear her *dat* ask her *mamm* if she'd like a bouquet of wildflowers, but she didn't turn around. She kept her attention on her sons, who were still watching her quizzically.

"Why can't we go with you, *Mamm*?" Jacob hopped onto the porch step, then cocked his head to the side. "You look—different."

"*Gut* different or bad different?"

Jacob shrugged, but Joseph jumped to his rescue. "*Gut*. Of course. You always look *gut*, *Mamm*. Even that time you fell in Nick's trough."

Hoping to avoid the retelling of that story, Deborah pulled her purse strap over her shoulder and squatted down in front of Jacob and Joseph. "Be sure and take your toothbrushes and a change of clothes to your cousin's house."

"We don't need clean clothes," Jacob reasoned. "We'll just get them dirty again, and that's more work for you."

"We already have everything set out in our packs, by the front door." Joseph put his arms around her neck, then kissed her cheek, reminding Deborah of the night before, of kissing her own *mamm*.

Jacob tugged on his *bruder*'s arm. "Come on. We gotta show Christopher our frogs."

"Be back in fifteen minutes," Mary called after them.

Nick had been talking to her parents about the goats. Great. They had two topics of conversation to cover on this supposed date—goats and children. He nodded toward the buggy, and she walked in that direction, suddenly feeling clumsy and self-conscious and as if she were sixteen again.

But she looked up and saw her *mamm* and *dat* and Mary, and that helped to settle her nerves. She waved and they waved back and smiled, as if this was a good idea. As if it wasn't a farce. Which was okay. Her parents looked pleased. Even Mary looked happy with the turn of events.

It didn't really matter what Nick thought of her— whether he liked her more or less after their first date. Her family knew her best. They'd been through the very worst with her, and still they loved her. What more did a woman need?

She pushed her fears and insecurities behind her and turned to face the man driving the buggy. With a resolve she didn't quite feel, she shook away the thought that this was her first date in seven years. She pushed down the memory of the terrible feeling of rejection she'd experienced when Gavin had told her he was leaving for Chicago. It didn't matter. None of that mattered.

It was time to step out of the past and live in the here and now.

Even if that meant going on a fake date with a man who could push her buttons better than a six-year-old. Her expectations for the evening were low enough that she didn't think she'd be disappointed—unless she had to wash the dinner dishes. That would be a disappointment for sure and certain.

Nick tugged at the collar of his shirt and tried to focus on directing his mare. "Get on, Big Girl."

"That's her name? Big Girl?"

"What's wrong with it?"

"Nothing. I didn't say anything was wrong with it."

He glanced her way, but he did not need to look at pretty Deborah Mast while he was driving. He might drive into the ditch. That would be a fine story to tell his siblings. Somehow they'd caught on to the fact that he had a date, and he was pretty sure there would be a thorough interrogation the next time they were all together.

"She's big for a mare, and—"

"She's a girl." Deborah's laughter spilled out. He liked the sound of it, though he'd never tell her that. She spent enough time laughing at him. No need to encourage her.

"What is so funny?"

"It's just that, well, you named your blue heeler Blue."

"And?"

"I just figured you might have named your chestnut mare Chestnut." She pressed her fingers to her lips, but it didn't stop her laughter.

"I get it." He sat back, resettled his hat and tried to

pretend he was hurt. "You're making fun of the guy who doesn't have an imagination."

"Now, I did not say that." She hesitated, then added, "But it sounds like maybe you've heard it before."

"Indeed."

"Tell me."

"Let's see…" He ran his fingers along his jawline. He'd shaved for the date because it seemed like the polite thing to do. He shaved every other day, and always in the morning, but he'd made a special effort for Deborah. It might be a fake date, but she was still a woman who deserved to be treated as if she was on a real date.

"I once named a tabby cat Tabby."

"You did not."

"Yup. There was another calico barn cat that I named—"

"Calico."

"You got it."

"I think you're making that up."

"I'm not." He shrugged. "Seemed to make sense to me."

"When you do marry, you might want to let your *fraa* name the children."

"*Boy* would be a fine name for a son."

She was laughing again and laid a hand on his arm. "Stop. You're giving me a stitch in my side."

"*Girl* for a *doschder.*"

Her laughter seemed to lift the tension from the buggy and drop it on the side of the road. They spent the next ten minutes talking about childhood pets.

When they entered Shipshewana proper, he said, "Thought we'd eat at Blue Gate—enjoy some *gut* Amish food."

"Oh." She blinked several times. "Okay."

But he drove past it, laughed when she pointed out that he'd done so and parked in front of the pizza parlor. "My *bruder* David reminded me that you eat Amish food all the time. He suggested—"

"Pizza. Sounds *wunderbaar*."

By the time he'd set the brake on the buggy and thrown Big Girl's reins over the hitching post, Deborah was out of the buggy and standing beside him. "Have you eaten here since you've been back?"

"A couple times with my *bruder*'s family." He cupped her elbow, walked her to the entrance and then opened the door before she could. It was all coming back to him now—though it had been a long time since he'd been on a date. Still, it wasn't that hard.

1. Arrive on time.
2. Look your best.
3. Be a gentleman.
4. Make conversation the other person will be interested in.
5. Don't talk about previous relationships.

They walked to the front counter, studied the menu board and settled on a pizza that was half meat supreme, half veggie. With two glasses of iced tea, the total came to just a tad over twenty dollars. He was pulling the money from his wallet when Deborah slipped a ten-dollar bill onto the counter.

He didn't say anything in front of the cashier. But when they were seated with their drinks, he said, "Let me give you your ten dollars back."

"No way."

"I know we said this isn't real…"

"It isn't." She sipped her tea and smiled broadly at him. When he didn't respond, she leaned forward and said, "Takes the pressure off. Don't you think?"

"*Ya.* I guess so." Nick stared across the room, trying to remember what else was on his list of dating etiquette. He had actually written one out, in the back of his five-year-plan journal. He couldn't have explained why he did it, but lists made him feel better. They made him feel more in control. He'd even written out a list of topics to talk about. Unfortunately, he couldn't remember a single one.

The silence was quickly growing awkward when Deborah jumped in with, "Tell me about the goats."

"Oh, well. Let's see." He took a sip of his iced tea. "They're Nubian goats. But I guess you knew that."

"Not really. Why did you pick Nubians?"

"High fat content in their milk, which is a good thing."

Deborah smiled and rubbed the condensation off the side of her glass. "*Ya*, I bought skim milk by mistake once. My boys wouldn't have a thing to do with it."

"I'd like to add some Alpine goats, maybe next year. Top goats can produce two gallons a day."

"That much?"

"*Ya.* I wouldn't kid you."

Surprisingly, she seemed interested. She propped her elbow on the table and rested her chin in her hand. She looked pretty that way, and if he'd been an *Englischer* who carried a phone around twenty-four hours a day, he'd ask to take her picture.

"If I had the money and time to raise goats, I'd raise Angoras."

"Because of the mohair?"

"Yes!" She spread her hands out flat on the table. "I like to knit. It's just…you know, something I do. But if money and time weren't a problem, I'd love to raise my own goats for the hair, then learn to spin it."

"You could do that."

"I guess."

Her expression turned suddenly melancholy. He searched his mind for a way to bring back her earlier, lighter mood. Finally he settled on telling her how his lead doe, Bertha, would stand on the very top of the play area Jacob and Joseph had built, bleating loudly. "The others crowd around her until it looks as if they're posing for an *Englisch* photographer."

He described the work the boys had done and how they'd improved throughout the week. "No more blood," he murmured as the waitress dropped the large pizza pie between them.

His diet of leftovers and sandwiches must be affecting him more than he realized—the pizza looked like a gourmet meal, and the smell was *wunderbaar*. "I'm tempted to sit here a minute and just savor the smell."

"You go ahead." Deborah reached for a piece from the veggie side and slipped it on her plate. "I'm starved."

He liked that she seemed to enjoy the meal.

"What are you thinking about?"

"Nothing."

"Go ahead. Say it."

"Just that I like how you eat."

"How I eat?" She snagged a napkin and wiped at her face.

"I like that you're enjoying the meal."

"Is that unusual?"

"Some women don't. Some are so worried about their figure and such that they can't relax around food."

"It sounds like you speak from experience."

He nodded, but he didn't explain. Rule No. 5—*Don't talk about previous relationships*—had popped into his mind like a blinking neon light.

"I had a cousin who had an eating disorder." Deborah chose another piece, studied it and then took a good-sized bite. Reaching for her tea, she added, "We all knew Tabitha was thin, but we didn't realize that she *couldn't* eat, that she was struggling so. Later, after she'd been to a treatment place over in Middlebury, she told me that when she looks in the mirror, she actually sees a large person. She was probably ninety pounds at that point. Isn't that odd? How your thoughts about a thing can change the way you perceive that thing?"

And there it was—another quality he really liked about Deborah. She didn't shy away from serious topics. She didn't mind discussing the hard stuff, like when she'd taken him to task for thinking he knew how to raise twins.

"Why are you smiling?"

"I was just thinking how you speak your mind."

"My *bruder*'s wife, Mary—she's probably my closest friend—she told me that I can be intimidating."

"I'm not intimidated."

"Gut."

Nick sighed. "Better to say what you're thinking than keep it inside. That only leads to trouble."

Deborah waited patiently, but he changed the subject.

They spoke of summer and crops and festivals. Finally, Nick realized he couldn't eat another bite. "Want to go and walk down the Pumpkinvine Trail a bit?"

"I'd love to."

The sun was just beginning to lower as he pulled the buggy into the small parking area at County Road 850. Deborah stood in front of Big Girl and pulled a carrot from her apron pocket.

"Have you been carrying that around all night?"

"Nein. I asked the cashier if I could snag a couple

from the salad bar." She dropped another piece of carrot into his hand. "Go ahead. Spoil your mare. Everyone does."

He laughed and fed the carrot to Big Girl, then assured the mare they'd be back soon.

They walked down the trail, passed other couples and families, even stopped to try and identify a few plants. Together, they enjoyed the summer day coming to an end. Nick almost reached for her hand. He almost let himself forget that this wasn't real.

It was when they were driving back toward home that she brought up their dating arrangement. "So, your family knows, about us, I mean?"

"That we're fake dating? *Nein.* They think it's real. It's not that I lied, but I didn't correct their assumptions."

"And why is that?"

"Honestly? I was worried if I let on that this is some convoluted plan of yours—"

"Thank you very much."

"Then someone might mention it to someone else, who might mention it to your folks, and then you'd be right back in the same place you were."

"Danki." Her voice was soft, sincere.

"You don't have to thank me, Deborah. When I took the time to consider your plan, it made sense for me, too. My family hassles me probably as much as yours hassles you."

"I doubt that very much."

He laughed. "Okay, well, maybe half as much."

"That's possible." She hesitated, then asked, "So why don't you date—for real date, I mean?"

He sighed deeply. Somehow, he'd known this was going to come up, but he was hoping it wouldn't be on their first fake date. Still, probably better to get it out of the way.

"I'm sure you've heard that I was to be married when I was living in Maine."

"I did hear that. Someone mentioned it at a church social. What happened?"

He was glad he was driving, that he had an excuse to not look directly at her. "Olivia changed her mind… sort of a runaway Amish bride."

"Did she actually run away?"

"She did." He glanced at her, then back at the road. "Don't look so horrified. It's a little funny now that I think about it."

"Seriously? It doesn't still…sting?"

"Well, yes. It does. But I can also see the humor in it. Rather than speak to me, she caught a bus to Tennessee. That's a little desperate, don't you think?"

"I'm so sorry, Nick. You didn't deserve to have that happen to you."

Many people had tried to cheer him up about what happened, but he wasn't sure he'd ever had someone commiserate with him so sincerely. Perhaps that was because Deborah knew a little about being rejected.

He cleared his throat. "My *bruder* told me a little about your situation."

"I was quite the topic of conversation my first year back." She drummed her fingers against the purse in her lap. "I suppose I deserved it. I was a living caution- ary tale for every Amish girl who stepped out with an *Englischer*."

"You cared for him, this *Englischer*?"

"I did. I thought he was the one." She stared out the window.

"And now? Do you still think that?"

"Nein." She turned to face him. "Anyone who could turn their back on Jacob and Joseph… They aren't the kind of person that I could love and make a life with."

"Sounds like you're over him."

"Oh, *ya*. Most definitely. I don't pine for Gavin anymore. When I think back to those days, it's almost as if it all happened to someone else."

"It's his loss, Deborah. Your boys—they're a handful, but they're *gut* boys. I can't imagine walking away from my own children."

"To be fair, he never met them. As soon as he learned I was pregnant, he legally terminated his parental rights."

"Wow."

"Yup. And then he left the area. Sort of like your runaway bride."

"I don't understand people sometimes."

A quiet settled around them, but it wasn't an uncomfortable silence. He was thinking about what strength it took to walk away from that type of rejection and what courage it took to go home.

To admit your mistakes and ask forgiveness.

To raise two boys on your own in the manner you believed they needed to be raised.

Nick directed Big Girl down her parents' lane. He pulled to a stop in front of the house but made no move to get out of the buggy. How did one end a fake date? Was he supposed to kiss her?

Before he could decide, she opened the door and hopped out of the buggy. Leaning in, she said, "Best fake date I've ever had."

"Only fake date I've ever had."

"Me, too. Thanks, Nick."

"Thank you, Deborah." It all sounded rather formal in his ears. He just was not good at this sort of thing.

She waved, smiled, shut the door and hurried up the steps.

Driving home didn't take long, since he lived next door. But it was long enough for him to sink into a very familiar gloom. Their fake date had awakened him in some way. He realized that he didn't like being alone, not all the time.

Blue met him at the barn door. Nick unharnessed Big Girl, stabled her and then headed into his house. It was pitch-dark inside, and he had to fumble around for the battery-powered lantern he kept on the kitchen counter. Its light seemed to mock him, accentuating just how bad his kitchen looked. In truth, the house was barely habitable and in desperate need of remodeling.

The house was lonely. *He* was lonely.

He couldn't consider seriously dating. Who would date him? Who would be willing to wait until he had the fields cultivated, the barn restored and the herd built up? He stood there, in the light of the single lantern with Blue at his feet, and wondered if his five-year plan might be wrong.

Because at that moment, five years—one thousand, eight hundred and twenty-five days—seemed like a very long time to wait to date. He was an idiot. He'd thought he could keep his heart wrapped up and tucked away, like the set of good dishes packed away in the barn.

Walking over to the sink, he filled a glass with tap water and stood at the window drinking it. He could just make out a light in the upstairs room of the Mast farm. Was it Deborah's room? Had she enjoyed the night? He hadn't even asked her.

She'd seemed to enjoy herself.

He readied for bed, his thoughts filled with her laughter and smile and direct way of looking at him. Deborah would make someone a fine *fraa*. Someone who was ready to marry. But she wouldn't want to wait five years. The boys would be eleven years old by then. They deserved to have a father now.

They deserved someone who would make them a priority.

He was very certain of one thing—that someone wasn't him. He'd make a terrible father. Maybe if he could start when they were babies, he could learn as they grew. The last week with Jacob and Joseph had proven that he didn't know a thing about raising young boys. He'd thought it would be easy!

Nick shook his head, climbed into bed and tried to put thoughts of the woman next door out of his mind.

He didn't succeed. Instead, he came up with a *wunderbaar* idea for their second fake date. She'd love it. Maybe he could be a good influence on her. Just because he was waiting five years didn't mean she should. Maybe she'd realize dating wasn't so horrible, and then she could find a real romantic interest and date that person.

That was the ticket.

It was a solid plan, and plans were what made things work. A smile on his face, Nick fell into a deep sleep. Unfortunately, his dreams were peppered with images of Deborah and the boys and a future that wasn't his to claim.

Chapter Six

For Deborah, the next week went too well, if that was possible. It wasn't that the boys didn't seek and find trouble. They most certainly did. It was more that Nick seemed to be handling things on his own.

When Jacob and Joseph managed to get into a mud fight after Monday's rain, Nick had them take off their shirts, scrub them clean in his sink and then hang them on the line. By the time they arrived back home, they were cleaner than when they left. Even more surprising, Nick did not show up on her doorstep when Jacob managed to cut his hand attempting to leap over a barbed-wire fence. Instead, Nick cleaned and bandaged the wound as well as Deborah could have, pinned a note to Jacob's shirt outlining what he'd done, and insisted the boy explain to her how it had happened.

Jacob did, in fine dramatic detail, ending with, "I'm supposed to tell you how it won't happen again."

"Is that so?"

"I can't tell the future, *Mamm*."

"Do you think that's what Nick meant?"

They were sitting on the back porch. She'd sent Joseph out to look for eggs in the chicken house so she could have a word with Jacob privately. The boys exchanged a look that said they'd tell each other everything once they were together again.

"Do you think Nick was expecting you to see into the future?"

"I guess not."

"So, what do you think he meant?"

Jacob pulled a piece of grass growing near the porch steps and stuck it in his mouth, something he'd probably seen the older boys do. He chewed on it a minute, then passed it from the right side to the left. "Nick seems to think that I get hurt a lot because I go too fast."

"Mmm-hmm."

"But isn't fast a good thing?"

"Sometimes it can be."

"He also said that I don't stop and consider what might happen."

Deborah felt an old flare of defensiveness rise up in her. The boy was six. True, he was about to turn seven. Also true, he did go too fast, and he most certainly did not think things through. Still, was it Nick's place to tell her son those things?

Jacob stood, brushed off his pants and tossed the piece of grass onto the ground. Moving to a lower step, he faced Deborah and put his small hands on her shoulders. "He could be right. I'm going to test out this theory."

"Test out this theory..." When had he started talking like an adult?

"For one week, I'll try to go slower and more carefully—which I have to tell you doesn't sound like much fun."

Deborah tried to hold back a grin.

"But the medicine he poured in my cut wasn't fun, either, so maybe it'll even out."

"That sounds like a mature decision."

"Only one week," he reminded her. "If I still get hurt, then I might as well go as fast and recklessly as I want."

He kissed her cheek, then took off in search of his *bruder*.

Deborah was left feeling proud of her son and more than a little discombobulated. Later that night, as she pulled out her knitting, she replayed the conversation in her mind. What about it had bothered her so much?

"You're frowning at that baby yarn as if you don't like it very much."

"Oh, I like it." She fingered the variegated yarn—pink, yellow, blue and green. What was there not to like? She remembered when she'd made something similar for her own boys. Now she knitted for new babies born into their church family, but not so much for Jacob and Joseph. Maybe a hat or scarf, but other than that, they had insisted that they'd rather stick to regular guy clothes.

"They're not babies anymore."

"Indeed. Jacob and Joseph are turning into fine boys."

"I rather miss the baby days." She ran her fingers over the yarn, sighed and finally picked up her knitting needles. This blanket wasn't going to knit itself.

"You'll have children again, Deborah. I suspect Jacob and Joseph will have many siblings. Don't be worrying about that."

Deborah threw a skeptical look at her *mamm* but managed to keep her opinions on that subject to herself.

"Are you and Nick going out again this Saturday?"

A subject she was even less eager to talk about.

"Um…I think so. Say, I think I'll have a cup of tea. Can I bring you one?"

"That would be *wunderbaar*."

Her *dat* had retired early, as he often did these days. Upstairs she heard a thump, followed by laughter. The boys were supposed to be reading, but Deborah suspected they usually spent the twenty minutes before bed having a pillow fight. She missed cuddling them, reading to them. Now when they sat together with a book, the boys insisted on sounding out the words themselves.

She made the cups of tea and added the tin of oatmeal cookies to the tray. When her *mamm* had set aside her quilting and chosen a cookie, she sat back, looked at Deborah and said, "You might as well tell me. It's plain as the apron over your dress that something is bothering you."

"The boys are doing well over at Nick's."

"He's been a real blessing to this family, for sure and certain."

"Sure. I guess."

"But…"

"I don't know. When the boys were younger, I longed for an hour to myself. Now I have no idea what to do with it…let alone an entire morning." She sipped her tea and scowled at the tin of cookies. She used to do the baking for her *mamm*, but she wasn't needed in the kitchen any more than she was needed with the boys.

"It's normal to feel a little at loose ends when you're in between *bopplin*."

"And what if I don't have other children?" She held up her hand to stop her mother's protest. "I know you believe I will, but what if I don't? What am I supposed to do every day?"

It sounded ridiculous even to her ears.

Instead of arguing, her *mamm* nodded in under-standing. "Your situation is a bit unique for an Amish woman."

"Exactly. Most women my age, women I know, have their hands so full that they're overwhelmed. Even Mary is busy, what with the move and helping with Simon's business."

Her *bruder* Simon was a farmer, like most Amish men, but he also offered tours of his farm. Mary handled most of those details. They hoped that the move to Middlebury would increase the number of tours they could do. Mary had shared with Deborah that they made more from the tours than they did from the crops. Since Mary wasn't able to have any more children, she'd become a real partner to Simon.

"No one is useless in this world who lightens the burden of someone else, and you have lightened my burden for sure and certain this last year."

"But…"

"But now that your father's health has stabilized…"

"You don't need me like you did."

"Extra hands make lighter work, Deborah. You're a *gut* cook and a *gut* cleaner, too."

"I learned from the best." Deborah meant it as a compliment, but it was followed by such a heavy sigh that even she heard the despair in her voice. "I honestly don't know what's wrong with me."

"*Gotte* made us each with unique abilities and talents. I love to quilt, but you're one of the best knitters that I know."

Deborah glanced down at the yarn in her hands and then shrugged. "I like knitting. I always have."

"You know, I hear the yarn shop in town is looking for part-time help."

Deborah nearly choked on the piece of cookie she'd popped in her mouth.

"It's only an idea."

"That I get a job? That's absurd, *Mamm*. I need to be here, with the boys."

"Maybe. But summer will be over before we know it, and then they'll be in school all day. If you don't think you'll be married by then…"

Now Deborah spilled her tea. "*Mamm*, why would you even say a thing like that?"

"Because I'm a bit mischievous." She leaned forward and handed Deborah a napkin to soak up the spilled tea. "It's okay if you don't feel that way about Nick yet. Sometimes love comes on slowly."

Deborah didn't know how to answer her mother. She had the sudden urge to confess that Nick wasn't really interested in her, but she wasn't ready for that conversation yet. So instead, she said, "I guess. But working in a shop… I don't know even one *mamm* with young children who does that."

"As we said, your situation is unique. You're in an in-between place right now, Deborah. It doesn't mean that *Gotte*'s done with you, only that you can't see His path for you yet."

That was the understatement of the year. "You think I should apply for the job?"

"I think you should consider it. Or maybe you'd rather serve pie at the Blue Gate."

"I would *not* rather do that."

Her *mamm* laughed. "Plain and Simple Yarns sounds like a better fit."

Did it? Another thud sounded from upstairs. Deborah stuck her knitting back in her bag. Jacob and Joseph might be growing up before her eyes, but they still needed tucking into bed. "On that note, I'm off to check on the boys. Perhaps an early night for myself will set things right."

But sleep didn't come so easily.

Should she apply for the job?

Could she work and still be a *gut mamm*?

Nick would probably make a list of pros and cons. Actually, that wasn't a bad idea. She tossed off the covers, found her journal, a pen and her night-light. Her *dat* had given her the battery-operated lamp when he'd caught her reading beneath the covers with a flashlight. "Better on your eyes," he'd explained, patting her shoulder.

She made a list. It didn't take long. There wasn't much to put on the con side. After all, if she found that working at the shop was too much or that the boys were suffering because she wasn't there, she could quit. And the truth was that the boys probably wouldn't notice. They loved spending mornings over at Nick's—the single hour having expanded to lunch. Soon she'd need to pay him for babysitting.

Only they weren't babies.

And he wasn't "sitting" with them. He was working with them. He was doing the things a father would do. Things that Deborah was ill-equipped to do.

Nick might not be genuinely interested in her, but he was a *gut* neighbor, a *gut* friend to her boys. She should be grateful for that.

And she should apply for the job at the knit shop, even if the very thought of doing so set her stomach to churning. She tossed from side to side, knowing she needed to sleep. Finally, she flipped onto her back and stared up at the ceiling. And there she found her answer, something her *mammi* used to say.

Her *dat*'s *mamm* had lived with them for several years when Deborah was a young teen. She was fond of proverbs—biblical and otherwise.

A merry heart doeth good like a medicine, but a broken spirit drieth the bones…from Proverbs.

The last cow closes the door…from her grandfather.

Oiled machinery runs smooth…just something people used to say.

That was often her answer when they questioned her. "Oh, it's just something people used to say." Deborah and her *schweschdern* had often rolled their eyes at *Mammi*'s sayings. Her *schweschder* Belinda had threatened to stitch them into pillowcases. *Mammi*'s pillowcases. They'd been sure *Englischers* would snap them up at The Mercantile. Unfortunately, hand-stitching letters onto cotton had been a monotonous task for teenage girls. They'd given up before they'd finished the second example.

But the sayings had worked their way into Deborah's heart. Now she thought of one that her *mammi* often repeated to Deborah's *bruders*.

Common sense is often wisdom clothed in work clothes.

Just maybe, it was time for Deborah to put on her work clothes.

The next day passed quickly, and Saturday morning seemed to arrive in a blink.

Her boys had planned to spend the day with Deborah's *schweschder*. Since Belinda lived on the far side of Shipshe—a good eight miles away—they only saw each other once or twice a month. Belinda and her husband had six girls. Jacob and Joseph enjoyed pretending that they didn't want to spend a day with six girls.

"They play the stupidest games, *Mamm*." Jacob extended his arms and pretended to swing a bat. "Why don't girls like normal games, like baseball?"

"Some girls do."

"Janie tried to braid my hair." Joseph shook his head in confusion as he finger-combed his bangs.

"She is only four. Perhaps next time you could distract her with—"

"Oh, look. They're here!" Both boys dashed off toward Belinda's buggy, any reservations about spending the day with six girls forgotten.

Belinda leaned out and hollered, "I need to get back to make lunch. Tell *Mamm* I'll visit when I bring them home this afternoon."

Deborah stood there, waving after them, and then hurried inside to prepare for her date. Nick had stopped by the day before and suggested that Deborah wear something she didn't mind getting dirty for their Saturday outing. He'd also asked if they could move the time to late morning. When she'd raised an eyebrow at the question, he'd only said, "Trust me," and walked off whistling.

He was whistling a lot these days.

She had no idea what that was about.

"I've never seen that dress before." Nick smiled at her as he held open the buggy door.

"Because I only wear it for cleaning." She gave him a pointed look. "Someone told me to dress down."

"Regardless, the blue fabric is causing your eyes to sparkle."

"I think that's my wariness shining through."

Nick laughed. He was feeling *gut* about this plan. If he was attracted to Deborah, then certainly other Amish men would be, too. It was only a matter of them getting to know her, of coaxing her off that farm. She'd find a proper beau, be in an authentic relationship, and he could go back to his five-year plan.

"What's the surprise?" she asked as Big Girl trotted down the lane and out onto the main road.

"Wouldn't be much of a surprise if I told you."

"Uh-huh." She sat up straight, peering out the window. "Seems like the same road we drove down last time. Taking me back to the pizza place?"

"Nope."

"You wouldn't have told me to wear an old dress for that."

"Nope."

"You're being quite mysterious, Nicholas Stoltzfus."

"Yup. Trust me. If you don't enjoy the outing, you can pick next week's destination." Only if things went well, there wouldn't be another fake date. "Tell me about your week."

She worried her thumbnail for a moment and finally shrugged. "I applied for a job yesterday."

"Seriously?"

"Yes. It was my *mamm*'s idea. I've been a bit out of sorts lately."

"Why is that?" He'd thought he'd done a *gut* job with Jacob and Joseph. He hadn't even panicked when Jacob had cut his finger. "Am I doing something wrong with the boys? Because you're right… Twins aren't as easy as one might think."

She laughed at that. He liked that he could make her laugh. He relaxed when the worry lines between her eyes faded.

"Quite the opposite. It's strange having an entire morning to myself. I feel like I should be doing more…"

"My *mamm* says that keeping a neat house is like threading beads on a string with no knot."

"Your *mamm* sounds like a wise woman."

"No doubt."

"But the thing is that I don't have a house to keep neat. My *mamm* does that. I help, of course. But there isn't enough work for the both of us. She shoos me away most days, or makes up something that doesn't really need to be done, like painting the fence around the garden."

"I noticed that. I thought maybe the boys had done it."

"Can you imagine my boys with paint?"

Nick gave a mock shudder, and she laughed again.

"Tell me about this job."

"My *mamm* encouraged me to apply at the knit shop in town. I'll find out next week if I've been chosen for the position."

He could see she was conflicted about working outside the home. "You're a *gut mamm*, Deborah. You're doing an admirable job raising boys that will grow into fine young men."

He thought she might tease him for saying that, since he'd given her such a hard time when they'd first met. She didn't. Instead, she stared out the window and returned to worrying her thumbnail.

"We're here."

He pulled into the Shipshewana Outdoor Market parking area and directed Big Girl to the back of the lot, where several other buggies were parked. The horses had been unharnessed and released into an adjacent field.

"Why are we here? Are we going in that van?"

"Trust me. Remember?"

"Uh-huh."

But she suddenly looked very wary. Other Amish couples were climbing into the van—all chattering and wearing older clothes. It seemed everyone knew where they were going except Deborah.

"It's definitely not an old folks' tour," she whispered as they neared the van.

Nick was pleased to see that the couples were probably close to her age. And some didn't seem to be couples at all, but rather friends.

She turned on Nick before they were within earshot of the others.

"What's this about? And don't give me that *trust me* line again. I hate surprises."

"Seriously?"

"Sort of. Today I do."

"We're going kayaking."

"Kayaking?"

"I heard from my *bruder* that a group meets here every Saturday at noon. They travel over to Bristol, rent kayaks and spend a few hours going down the river." Unable to resist, he reached out and tucked a wayward lock of hair into her *kapp.* "Come on. What's the worst that could happen?"

"I could fall in."

"Water won't hurt you."

"I could drown."

"Can't you swim?"

"Yes. I can swim." She rolled her eyes, then marched toward the van.

He'd found something Deborah Mast was afraid of, and it wasn't kayaking. She avoided social situations. Had she always been that way, or only since her return from Ohio? Was she afraid that people were judging her, or was it simply a matter of being out of practice?

Nick paid the driver ten dollars and followed Deborah to the back of the bus. Bristol was only a fifteen-minute ride away, but most people preferred not to take their horse and buggy that far. Also, there wasn't a good place at the park to leave a horse for several hours. With each person paying five dollars, the driver certainly made enough for it to be worth their trouble, and the man who ran the outdoor market—which wasn't open on Saturdays—had given his permission for them to leave the horses and buggies in his field.

As they drove toward Bristol, everyone introduced themselves. Nick didn't think he'd remember all the names, but it didn't matter. He'd brought Deborah here so she could meet more people her age, and so she could learn to be comfortable in a group of singles again.

Sitting beside her on the van seat, he had to remind himself that he'd brought her here so she could find a proper beau. He didn't think sharing that with Deborah was a good idea, though. Instead, he struck up a conversation with two brothers sitting across the aisle, who looked to be Deborah's age. By the time they pulled into the parking lot of Fluid Fun Paddlesports, it felt as if they all knew each other.

The kayaks were a rainbow of colors—orange and blue and yellow and red. Deborah seemed to relax once they were paired off again, choosing their kayaks and paddles and vests.

"I'm supposed to wear this?" She held up the life preserver.

"*Ya*. Keeps you from drowning if you fall in."

"I was kidding before. I can swim."

"But it's required…see?" He pointed toward the sign

near the rental kiosk, then helped her into the orange vest, adjusting the straps and laughing when Deborah pretended she couldn't breathe. Standing that close to her, breathing in the smell of lilac and soap, he felt momentarily light-headed. It was probably just that he hadn't had a proper breakfast. There were several snack bars positioned along the river, so he'd remedy that soon enough.

Fifteen minutes later, they were in a two-person kayak, and a teenage *Englisch* kid was showing them how to use the paddles, how to turn the kayak and how to back up. After a brief tutorial, he told them to be careful and that lifeguards would be patrolling the river if they needed help.

Deborah was tentative at first, but it didn't take her long to learn the paddling motion. They practiced in the middle of the river, and then when they were more confident, Deborah directed the kayak to a cluster of reeds, where they paused to watch turtles climb up onto a log. Twice they nearly collided with other kayakers, which resulted in everyone laughing and attempting to back up.

When she splashed him with water, he knew that she was truly enjoying herself. They paddled around the bend in the St. Joseph River and pulled up to a snack bar nestled on the bank of the river.

"Hungry?"

"Starving."

He hopped out of the kayak and pulled it to the edge of the water, then reached for her hand. And in an instant, the moment went from light and carefree to something different. Deborah's eyes met his. Nick felt disoriented, off balance, even. Then she smiled, lifted her dress so that it wouldn't get any wetter than it already was and sashayed up to the snack bar.

Was she flirting with him?

Good grief. He was an idiot. He was going about this all wrong. He needed to remind her that this wasn't a real relationship. He needed to remind himself of the very same thing. Nick crammed his hat down on his head, hoping it might change the direction of his thoughts, and hurried to catch up.

They both ordered hot dogs and chips and bottles of water and sat on the grass, looking out over the river.

"This was a *gut* idea."

"It was?"

Deborah had taken a large bite of the hot dog, and now she started laughing and nearly choked on the food.

"What's so funny? Do I have moss in my hair? Water stains on my shirt?"

She caught her breath and took a drink from the bottle of water she'd purchased. This time she'd insisted on paying for his lunch, though he had no idea how she managed to have any extra money.

"What was funny was the look on your face when I complimented you."

"Oh, *ya*. That was a big surprise."

He bumped her shoulder with his and bit into his own chili dog. How could a chili dog taste so good? It was probably the same cheese, chili, bun and meat that he'd tried to make at home last week. His had tasted like cardboard. Now, sitting on the banks of the St. Joseph River, sitting next to Deborah in the summer sunshine, the food tasted like a gourmet meal.

When she leaned toward him to point out a family of ducks paddling across the river, Nick had an urge to put his arm around her. Then she looked up at him, eyes wide, lips slightly parted. All he had to do was lean forward an inch, maybe two. All he had to do was put his fears and insecurity behind him and kiss her.

Instead, he jumped up, knocking his water bottle over and dropping his paper plate and napkins.

"What's wrong?"

"Nothing."

"Nothing?"

"Just…um…decided I'd like some ice cream." He started walking away from her, walking backward so he could keep talking to her. "Can I get you some?"

"You want to buy me ice cream?"

"Sure. I'll just…"

"Surprise me." The words were soft, and she was looking at him as if he'd lost his mind.

He had lost his mind. He was supposed to be scoping out a new beau for her, a real beau. He was not supposed to be falling for Deborah Mast.

He ordered two double dips of ice cream, getting a variety of flavors since he had no idea what she liked. Passing the money to the teen working the cash register, he noticed his hand shaking slightly.

Get a grip, man.

Pulling in a deep breath, he accepted the change, tossed it into the tip jar and carried the ice cream to Deborah.

"Mint chocolate chip with strawberry? Interesting combination…"

"Uh, *ya*. Or you could have this one…" He thrust the second cone toward her.

"What is that?"

"I have no idea."

She stepped closer to him, accepted the mystery ice cream and took a bite. "Butter pecan on top, and I'm pretty sure that's chocolate chip on bottom. Pretty *gut*, too." Smiling and looking intently into his eyes, she wagged the cone back and forth. "Let me know if you want to trade."

Then she made her way back to the water, balancing easily as she stepped into the kayak and walked to the back seat. Turning, she plopped down and took another bite of her ice cream.

Nick practically groaned.

He could not be falling for this woman. She was all wrong for him. She was independent and strong-willed and the *mamm* of two boys.

She was beautiful and made him laugh.

But most importantly, she was everything that his five-year plan did not allow for. He pushed the kayak back into the water, hopped in and sat facing Deborah. The kayak slowly drifted to the middle of the river as they enjoyed their ice cream.

The silence wasn't awkward or strained.

It was peaceful, except for the thoughts zipping around in his mind. How attached was he to that five-year plan? Nick knew that plan was a crutch. He'd developed it when Olivia had first run away, when he'd decided to leave Maine behind and return home. He'd made the decision to throw his life into work and to leave relationships to other people. In that way, he was no better than Deborah. He was avoiding getting hurt, and he had a feeling that she was, too.

The important question was whether he was willing to take a chance. The woman eating ice cream in the sunshine of a near-perfect June afternoon wasn't what he needed, but she might be everything that was missing in his life.

Chapter Seven

Deborah checked the messages on the machine in the phone shack Monday afternoon. Her stomach flipped when she heard the voice of the manager of Plain and Simple Yarns asking her to return the call. Pulling in a steadying breath, she did, and Maggie Jennings offered her the job. She would start out working mornings, three days a week, and they'd add more hours as needed if she wanted them.

Her first day of work was Wednesday.

She was a wreck.

What if the boys needed her? What if her *mamm* needed her? What if her *dat* had another heart episode?

"Your parents will ring the bell if they need anything," Nick had assured her when he met her buggy as she'd pulled down his lane. "And you don't have to worry about the boys. They're helping me in the vegetable garden today, plus doing their regular chores with the goats."

Jacob and Joseph looked up from the garden and waved at her. Not so long ago, they would have run to see her, but with Blue watching them with adoring eyes—and given the dirt fight that seemed to be going on—they didn't have time for such childish things. The thought depressed her even more.

"You said you wanted this." Nick stepped closer to the buggy, putting his hands on the open window.

She looked down at those hands—a farmer's hands, complete with calluses, a scratch or two and, of course, a suntan. She looked at his hands and wondered what they'd feel like touching her face.

"Hey. Are you okay?"

She jerked as if a bee had stung her. "Of course. I'm just having an emotional morning. It happens when you're a parent."

"I would know nothing about that."

"Lucky you."

"I would say 'break a leg,' but that doesn't sound appropriate for working in a yarn shop."

"Please don't wish that on me." Her laughter was weak, but the kindness in Nick's eyes did a lot to calm her heaving stomach.

"You can do this, Deborah. You'll be *gut* at it. And your family will be fine."

"Right. I know that."

"Try to enjoy the time off the farm."

"Uh-huh. Okay." She plastered on a smile, then called out to Rhapsody and turned the buggy toward town. In spite of her completely unnecessary side trip to Nick's, she made it to the shop ten minutes early. She tied her mare to a hitching post in a shady spot. Rhapsody was a five-year-old red roan with a white marking running from her forelock to her muzzle. Stopping to rub her on the white spot, Deborah whispered, "Back in a few hours. You're a *gut* horse."

The mare nodded in agreement.

Maggie Jennings was every bit as nice as she'd

seemed during the interview. She insisted that Deborah call her Maggie instead of Mrs. Jennings, was super patient when she had to explain the cash register procedure three times and didn't even get perturbed when Deborah tripped and spilled several baskets of wool yarn.

"I've been meaning to move those." Maggie cocked her head. She was probably only ten years older than Deborah. Her hair was brown streaked with blond. She was dressed in jeans and a button-down shirt that had the store's logo on the pocket. "Want to try your hand at creating a new display?"

"Me?"

"Sure. Let's see what you come up with. If we don't like it, we'll change it."

Deborah liked the *we* in that statement. She spent the next hour playing with the display until she came up with something that she thought looked appealing. Clearing off the top of a bookcase that held knitting books, she turned the round baskets on their sides and stacked them in a pyramid fashion. She secured the right and left sides with heavy ceramic bowls that she'd seen in the storeroom. The red wools went in one ceramic bowl, the purples in the other. The rest of the yarn went into the baskets, making a delightful palette of colors from light to dark.

"Wow."

"Do you like it?"

"Nope." Maggie shook her head, causing her long earrings to bounce back and forth. "I love it."

The last hour of her first day was busy. It seemed that lunch hour was a prime time for shopping. She only messed up two of the eight transactions.

"It gets easier every day, Deborah. I think you're a good fit for my shop."

"*Danki*… I mean, thank you."

"Honey, I'll take a thank-you in Amish or English. Now, I know you're anxious to get home and check on those boys, so off you go."

By the time Deborah walked out to Rhapsody, she was exhausted but also feeling more confident. She could do this. Knitting came naturally to her. She understood the different weights and could put together what kind of fiber worked best for each type of project. But more importantly, she had a pleasant boss.

Unfortunately, the satisfied feeling didn't last. She came home to find Jacob sitting at the kitchen table, holding an ice pack to the top of his head.

"What happened?"

"You know that thing we talked about?"

"Going slow and being careful?"

"Yeah. I sort of forgot."

Joseph was sitting at the table, watching his *bruder* with worried eyes. "Are you still seeing double?"

"What? You were seeing double? Do we need to go to the—"

"*Nein.*" Her *mamm* walked in holding a dust rag. "I checked the chart the doctor gave us last time."

"I can walk a straight line."

"He remembers his birthday," Joseph offered.

Jacob immediately perked up. "Speaking of birthdays—"

"Let's not. Why don't you tell me what happened?"

Jacob studied the ceiling as if what Deborah wanted or needed to hear was written there. "We were playing Frisbee with Blue. You remember that old Frisbee that *Onkel* Simon gave me? It's a bright orange with—"

Deborah sank into a chair opposite her sons. She motioned for Jacob to hurry along his story.

"Well, the Frisbee went up on the roof, and Blue was barking…"

"It went up on the roof? All by itself?"

"Maybe?" Jacob glanced to Joseph for help.

"Actually, no," Joseph clarified. "Remember? You said something like 'watch how high I can throw this.'"

"You're not helping, *bruder.*"

Deborah closed her eyes and prayed for patience.

Jacob cleared his throat and tried again. "Turns out I'm *gut* with a Frisbee. I can throw it quite high. After it went on the roof, we needed to get it down, and we didn't want to bother Nick. He was out in the field."

"You climbed on the roof?"

"Shimmied up the rain gutter, which would have been fine, except when I got up there, after I'd thrown the Frisbee down to Blue…"

"He caught it, too," Joseph piped in. "Blue is a *gut* catcher."

"My foot slipped, and down I went. Next thing I knew, Joseph was standing over me and Blue was licking my face."

"I made sure he could open his eyes and then ran to fetch Nick. He was not too happy."

"Nope. I'd say he would have grounded me if he could, so I guess it's a *gut* thing he's not our *dat.*"

Deborah winced at that. The boys seemed to be waiting to see whether she'd give them a Popsicle or a lecture. She stood, removed the ice pack and studied the red lump. At least it wasn't bleeding. He didn't seem to have a concussion. She supposed she should be grateful that he wasn't hurt any more seriously.

"You're lucky you didn't break anything."

"*Ya*, for sure, I am."

"And you should be ashamed for breaking your word to Nick. You promised him that you'd be careful."

"I wouldn't say I broke my word—"

"Stop talking."

Both boys sat up straighter, their eyes wider, their attention now focused completely on her.

In that moment, Deborah wondered if she'd somehow overcompensated for their not having a father. Had she been too lenient with them? Was this her fault?

"I want you to write an apology note."

Jacob groaned. "You know my writing is terrible. Couldn't I just clean out the horse stall or something gross like that?"

"It will be neatly written, even if you have to copy it down more than once."

"I'll do one, too," Joseph offered. "We'll do it together."

"Nope. This is Jacob's problem, and Jacob is going to handle it." She squatted in front of Jacob's chair. "I'm disappointed in you, son. You broke your promise, you probably scared a year off Nick's life, not to mention your *mammi*'s, and most importantly, you could have been seriously hurt."

He stared at the floor, no doubt unaccustomed to being lectured. For once, his confident, cocky smile was missing. That was a good start. Perhaps he'd feel real remorse and be more careful in the future.

But somehow, she didn't think it was going to be that easy.

It took great resolve, but Nick managed to wait until late afternoon before going over to Deborah's. Ostensibly, he still stopped by a couple times a week to update

John on how the goats were doing. He felt that excuse was wearing a bit thin. There was little to report on the goat front.

But Deborah's *dat* seemed to enjoy his visits.

He'd managed to avoid Bethany's offers of dinner. Somehow it felt like an invisible line he shouldn't cross. Deborah's mother meant well, but eating together felt too much like being one of the family. Since their outing on Saturday, he'd been arguing with himself as to whether his feelings toward Deborah were real or simply a product of his loneliness. At least he'd come to terms with the fact that he was lonely. He could have gone years—five years, to be exact—pretending that he was perfectly happy living alone on the farm. Now he accepted that simply wasn't the case.

His resolve to keep at least some amount of distance between himself and Deborah's family crumbled when he walked into the house and smelled dinner cooking. When Bethany once again invited him to stay for the meal, his mind went blank and he couldn't come up with an excuse that he would believe, let alone anyone else. Instead, he said he'd love to and then sat in the living room, discussing summer crops with John. "Say, it's awfully quiet around here. Where are the boys?"

John smiled and drummed his fingers against the rocking chair. "Jacob's in his room, writing an apology letter."

"An apology letter?"

"For this morning's incident."

"Ah." He couldn't think of anything else to say to that piece of news. When he'd seen Jacob lying on the ground, his first thought had been that Deborah would kill him—he was supposed to be watching the boys while she was at work. His second thought was that

Jacob apparently only learned by experience. "And Joseph?"

"Out spoiling my horses with carrots, mainly because Deborah said he couldn't help with the letter."

This time Nick simply nodded.

None of this was making sense to him, though. He hadn't asked for an apology letter.

"And Deborah's on the back porch, cleaning it as if spring had just arrived." He looked at Nick and winked. "She could probably use some help."

"Oh, *ya*. Sure. I'll go and see if there's anything I can do."

John waved him toward the kitchen. He walked into the room and stopped as the smells from what Bethany was cooking caused his stomach to grumble loudly.

Deborah's *mamm* looked at him and smiled. "Dinner will be ready in fifteen minutes."

"Fifteen minutes. Got it." He'd been to the Mast place many times in the last month. But he hadn't ever been on the back porch. No doubt he looked as confused as he felt.

"Through the mudroom," Bethany said as she checked the dish in the oven.

"Smells *gut*."

"Should taste even better."

A thump sounded from the back of the house.

Nick paused and breathed in deeply. "My house doesn't smell like this."

Bethany turned and studied him. "I suspect that being a bachelor has its advantages, but eating well isn't one of them."

"Probably you're right. Guess I'll just…" He headed toward the mudroom and walked through it and out onto the porch.

The porch stretched across the back of the house and was screened in all around. It looked like something out of a magazine—rocking chairs, bright-colored cushions, potted plants, even an old barrel turned over and made into a spot to play checkers.

Deborah was standing on a chair, whacking a broom against the ceiling, determined to knock down something Nick couldn't see.

"Need help with that...whatever that is you're doing?"

"Dusting cobwebs. Seems new ones pop up every day." She whacked the ceiling again, scowled at it, then hopped off the chair.

"Your *mamm* said dinner would be ready soon."

"Don't tell me you're finally going to try my *mamm*'s cooking?"

"She wore me down."

"I know that feeling."

"Plus, who can say no to chicken casserole and fresh bread?"

"I wouldn't." Deborah looked somewhat upset. Her eyes kept darting left and right, and she was still clutching the broom.

"Want to tell me what's troubling you?"

She didn't bother denying that something was bothering her. Instead, she sank onto a swing that looked out over the garden area. Nick could have sat in the chair next to her, probably should have, but she looked so forlorn. He sat beside her on the swing, pushed his foot against the porch floor and set the swing to rocking. He didn't rush her. Didn't question her. Just waited. He didn't know a lot about women, but his *schweschdern* had taught him to be patient and quiet when they were in a mood.

"I clean when I'm upset."

"*Ya?* I tend to work in the barn. There's always some unpleasant job there that needs doing."

"We have more in common than I would have thought." Deborah shook her head. "I do not know what I'm going to do with my son."

"Which one?"

"The one that's in trouble."

"Heard he's upstairs working on a letter."

"Yes, and when I told him he would write one, he suggested that he clean out the barn instead—so maybe your good work ethic is rubbing off on him."

"Ah."

"How was your day?" She turned and looked at him fully, as if she was quite interested.

Nick wasn't used to that type of scrutiny. He stared out at the garden, a smile forming on his lips. "Oh, just a normal Wednesday. Tended to the goats, cared for my horses, then worked in the fields. I had two *gut* helpers, so the morning passed quickly."

"Except one of your helpers happens to be quite accident-prone."

She began worrying her thumbnail with her forefinger. He put his hand on top of hers, intertwined his fingers with her fingers. It was a stupid thing to do, but Deborah looked as if she needed a bit of comfort. It wasn't like he'd reached over and kissed her, though suddenly that sounded like a fine idea, too.

"Jacob may be intent on learning things the hard way," he admitted, "but he is learning."

"Are you sure?"

And now she had tears in her eyes. One slipped out, and he reached up and thumbed it away. For the briefest moment, Deborah leaned into the palm of his hand, then she jumped up off the swing and began pacing back and forth in front of him.

"I don't know why I'm so emotional."

"It was a big day for you—new job and all. You probably didn't sleep well last night thinking about it."

"True."

"How did it go?"

"Well."

"*Ya?* That's *wunderbaar.*"

"Is it? While I was gone, my son fell off a roof. He could have…could have broken something." She turned away from him, faced the view of the garden and beyond that the fields and finally his place.

Nick stood and walked over to her, reached for her hand and pushed open the screen door. "Let's take a walk."

She rolled her eyes, but she didn't resist. Now that he was holding her hand, it seemed strange to drop it, so instead he again intertwined his fingers with hers. They walked up and down the rows of the garden, between the green beans and tomatoes and squash plants, breathing in the smell of summer. The garden was bordered with bright flowers that appeared to be nodding at them.

When she seemed to have control of her emotions, he cleared his throat and said, "It didn't happen because you were at work."

"I know that."

"Would have happened even if you'd been here."

Now she simply nodded.

"Doesn't make you a bad *mamm.*"

"But maybe I am a bad *mamm.* I enjoyed my morning away. I liked being away from my children." She pulled her hand from his and pinched off a few dead pansy blooms. "I don't think that's normal."

Get ready to relax and indulge with your FREE BOOKS and more!

Claim up to FOUR NEW BOOKS & TWO MYSTERY GIFTS – absolutely FREE!

Dear Reader,

We both know life can be difficult at times. That's why it's important to treat yourself so you can relax and recharge once in a while.

And I'd like to help you do this by sending you this amazing offer of up to FOUR brand new full length FREE BOOKS that WE pay for.

This is everything I have ready to send to you right now:

Try **Love Inspired® Romance Larger-Print** books and fall in love with inspirational romances that take you on an uplifting journey of faith, forgiveness and hope.

Try **Love Inspired® Suspense Larger-Print** books where courage and optimism unite in stories of faith and love in the face of danger.

Or **TRY BOTH!**

All we ask in return is that you answer 4 simple questions on the attached Treat Yourself survey. You'll get **Two Free Books** and **Two Mystery Gifts** from each series you try, *altogether worth over $20*! Who could pass up a deal like that?

Sincerely,

Pam Powers

Harlequin Reader Service

Treat Yourself to Free Books and Free Gifts.

Answer 4 fun questions and get rewarded.

We love to connect with our readers! Please tell us a little about you...

	YES	NO
1. I LOVE reading a good book.	◯	◯
2. I indulge and "treat" myself often.	◯	◯
3. I love getting FREE things.	◯	◯
4. Reading is one of my favorite activities.	◯	◯

TREAT YOURSELF • Pick your 2 Free Books...

Yes! Please send me my Free Books from each series I select and Free Mystery Gifts. I understand that I am under no obligation to buy anything, as explained on the back of this card.

Which do you prefer?

❏ **Love Inspired® Romance Larger-Print** 122/322 IDL GRDP
❏ **Love Inspired® Suspense Larger-Print** 107/307 IDL GRDP
❏ **Try Both** 122/322 & 107/307 IDL GRED

FIRST NAME	LAST NAME

ADDRESS

APT.#	CITY

STATE/PROV.	ZIP/POSTAL CODE

EMAIL ❏ Please check this box if you would like to receive newsletters and promotional emails from Harlequin Enterprises ULC and its affiliates. You can unsubscribe anytime.

LI/SLI-520-TY22

"Hmm…"

"You disagree? Because you know so much about raising children and what is and isn't normal."

He held up a hand to stop her argument. "Wasn't going to say either of those things. But I love my farm—love the fields, the animals, even the old house I live in."

"Okay."

"I still enjoyed our day on the river. Doesn't mean I love my farm any less."

"You're comparing my sons to a piece of land."

"I suppose I am."

She shook her head, but a smile was forming on her lips. "Maybe you're a bad farmer and I'm a bad *mamm*."

"Maybe."

"But you don't think so."

"I don't." He smiled broadly. "Tell me about your first day in the yarn shop."

As they walked back toward the house, she described her boss, the customers and the display she'd created.

"What was your favorite part of being there?"

"The smell."

"Ya?"

"Yarn has a smell about it that is earthy, clean… Why are you laughing?"

"Because that's what I like best about my barn."

Dinner was the best he could remember having in a very long time. The boys kept the conversation going, the food was delicious and Deborah's parents were a pleasant couple to be around. But Nick's attention kept drifting back to what Deborah had said on their walk.

Why did she put so much pressure on herself?

What was it like to raise children without a spouse to help?

Why had the boys' father walked out on her?

What kind of fool was the guy?

One man's loss is another man's gain... The saying popped into his mind, and he pushed it away. He was Deborah's friend, nothing more.

When the boys had cleared the table, placing all the dishes next to the sink, they stood next to their *mamm*.

"Can we go now?" Jacob asked. "It's the best time to catch frogs."

Joseph nodded in agreement. "We promise to go slow."

"And careful." Jacob shifted restlessly from one foot to the other.

"Not yet." Deborah stared at Jacob. When he only crossed and uncrossed his arms, she prompted him with, "You have something to give Nick."

"Oh. Right." He dashed out of the room, then called from the stairs, "I'm going slow."

He returned with a single sheet of paper that had been folded into a triangular football—the kind that Nick used to make when he was sitting through a math lesson and was bored.

Jacob stopped in front of Nick's chair, his expression now quite solemn. "I wrote this for you."

"Should I read it now?"

"*Ya.* Of course."

Nick unfolded the piece of paper, aware that everyone's eyes were on him. With a strength he didn't realize he had, he held in his laughter and kept his voice quite serious. "*Danki*, Jacob. That's a very nice apology letter."

Jacob's worried expression transformed into a grin, and he threw his arms around Nick. "I'm glad you liked it," he whispered, and then with a nod from their *mamm*, both boys were out the back door, across the porch and into the yard.

"Lots of energy there," John said.

"Oh, *ya.*" Bethany laughed. "They remind me of your *bruders,* Deborah."

Deborah's parents tried to do the dishes, but Deborah and Nick insisted they leave the kitchen cleanup to them. Nick ran the tap water until it turned hot, then plugged the sink and squirted in dish soap. Deborah had gone to the mudroom, and he wondered if she needed help with something. He turned off the water and went in search of her. She was standing at the door to the porch, watching her parents, who now sat in the same place that she and Nick had occupied an hour earlier.

But John's arm was around his wife's shoulders, and her head rested against him.

Deborah glanced up at Nick, smiled weakly, and they both went back to the kitchen. They spoke of summer and the boys' upcoming birthday and the goats and how quickly the days were passing until they began school. Nick told her that he was considering adding a few pigs to his menagerie, and Deborah tried to describe a new sweater pattern that she was going to knit for a fall display at the yarn shop. In other words, they shared their day.

For the first time in a very long time, Nick didn't think about the work still to be done at his place, or the progression toward his five-year plan, or how long they should continue their fake relationship. For the first time in a very long time, he didn't look forward or back. He simply enjoyed the moment, the setting sun on a June day and the presence of the beautiful woman standing beside him.

When it was time to go back to his place, he said

good-night and turned away, but Deborah pulled him back. "The note from Jacob, do you mind if I read it?"

"Not at all. He did a *gut* job." Pulling the note from his pocket, he handed it to her.

She unfolded the single sheet of paper, and he stepped behind her so that he could read it—again— over her shoulder.

> *Nick,*
> Mamm *said I must rite this note.*
> *Bcuz I brok my promise.*
> *I 4got to go slo.*
> *Sorry I climbed on your ruf and fell off.*
> *Blue is a* gut *dog.*
> *I'll try to do better.*
> *Jacob*

Deborah sighed heavily, refolded the note and handed it back to Nick.

"It's a *gut* note," he assured her.

"His spelling is terrible."

"*Ya.* I noticed that. But someone reminded me not that long ago that he's only six."

She rolled her eyes, but a smile replaced the worried lines on her face.

And that was enough to ease the ache in Nick's heart. He needed to know that Deborah was okay, that she wasn't worrying or sad. It didn't mean that he cared about her more than any other friend. It simply meant that they were important to one another, as they should be, as *gut* neighbors were.

Yup. That explained his relief and the fact that he whistled all the way home.

But once again he was confronted with a house that

was empty, in need of fresh paint, lonely. His mind insisted on comparing his kitchen to the one next door—no good smells, no lively discussions, no family. Then he glanced out the window at his porch, if it could even be described as that. There wasn't a chair or a plant or a pillow cushion in sight—just Blue, head on his paws, fast asleep.

He could remodel the house, adjust his plans to do it earlier than he'd scheduled. He could make it more hospitable. But he was honest enough with himself to know that new paint wouldn't ease the ache in his heart. Which left him wondering—what, exactly, would?

Chapter Eight

Jacob and Joseph turned seven on the fifth of July. Fortunately, it was a Tuesday, which meant that Deborah's work hours at the yarn shop didn't interfere with the birthday celebration.

Deborah had spoken to her *schweschder*-in-law twice to confirm plans. They'd all meet at Howie's Ice Cream at four in the afternoon. The treat might ruin the boys' appetite for dinner, but as Jacob pointed out, "Never hurts to eat dessert first. That way you have plenty of room for the important stuff."

She worried whether she should invite Nick, but that turned out to be a waste of worrying time. The boys had taken the liberty of inviting him.

"You should have asked me first." She licked her thumb and attempted to settle Jacob's cowlick.

He ducked away with a drawn-out *"Mamm..."* and a smile.

"Nick loves ice cream," Joseph explained. "It would have been rude to not invite him. Especially after Jacob let the pigs loose."

"Nick doesn't get mad anymore, but he gives us this look and somehow you just know you did the wrong thing." Jacob shrugged. "The pigs seemed to enjoy a run through the field."

True to his word, Nick had purchased a sow and three piglets. They'd arrived the week before. The boys were fascinated with them, which might explain why they came home every day in damp clothes. Apparently Nick insisted they wash the mud off themselves so that Deborah wouldn't have extra laundry. She suspected these washings turned into water fights, but she couldn't get very worked up about boys playing in the water on a hot summer day.

Nick arrived with his horse and buggy promptly at three thirty. After knocking on the front door, he called out, "Anyone want to ride with me?"

The boys dashed through the door with a shout and darted for his buggy.

Deborah followed the boys, then stopped halfway between Nick's buggy and her *dat*'s, uncertain which buggy to get into.

Nick stepped closer and lowered his voice. "We're still supposed to be fake dating, so you might want to…" He nodded toward his buggy.

"Oh, *ya*." She smiled up at him sweetly. "I almost forgot."

"Somehow, I don't think you did forget. After all, it was your idea to show me your yarn store last Saturday."

"I thought you wanted to buy yarn."

"And the week before that, you nearly killed me."

"Bicycling the Pumpkinvine Trail?"

"A lot of the Pumpkinvine Trail. What did we do… five miles?"

"Something like that."

"My legs are still sore." He winced with each step as they walked toward his buggy. She liked this side of

Nick—the casual, fun Nick. Why had she ever thought he was a grumpy old bachelor? He was actually a good-natured old bachelor.

Stopping at the back of his buggy, he lowered his voice and nodded toward the house. "Your parents are standing at the front door watching us. Should I kiss you?"

"You should not!" Heat blossomed in her face, but she was rather enjoying his teasing. Turning back to her parents, she called out, "Looks like you two are going to have a nice quiet ride."

Her *mamm* and *dat* stepped out onto the porch.

"It'll be like when we were courting, John."

"You can remember that?"

"Of course I remember." She swatted his arm. "And for suggesting that you don't, you can buy me a double scoop."

John winked at Deborah. "Your *mamm* knows how to keep me in line."

"Your parents have this marriage thing figured out."

Deborah looked at her parents again—now they were walking arm in arm.

When they were in the buggy, trundling down the lane and following her *dat*'s buggy, Nick returned to the subject of her parents. "You're lucky to have them living so close."

"Like in the next room?"

He laughed. "My parents moved to Tennessee, to help my *bruder* with his farm."

"What about your siblings?" She couldn't believe she hadn't asked him this. She'd been so focused on her own life, her own problems, that she realized she knew very little about him.

"You know David and Lydia."

"Sure."

"They're the only ones that stayed in the area."

"So why did you move back here?"

Nick shrugged. "Felt right to come back to where I'd been raised. I don't know anything about Tennessee, and I'd already tried living in a completely different place."

"What was Maine like?"

"Cold. Lots of snow. We had to shovel it off the roofs each year."

The boys, who had been uncharacteristically quiet, popped up and stuck their heads in between them.

"Did you ever try sliding off the roof?" Jacob asked.

"What did your animals do?" Joseph ran his fingers over the top of the seat. "I mean, were they okay in the cold?"

"We did not slide off the roof, as someone could have been hurt." Nick directed that comment to Jacob, who scratched his head, as if he'd never considered such a thing. "The animals are used to the cold for the most part, but Blue—well, that's why he lives inside with me. In Maine, it didn't feel right leaving him on the porch or in the barn."

"I'd like to have a dog that slept in my bed," Joseph declared.

"Oh, he's not in my bed." Nick laughed at the thought. "He sleeps on the floor beside my bed."

"That would work for me," Jacob said. "Can we get a dog, *Mamm*? For our birthday?"

Deborah put them off with "Maybe next year."

The boys sat back, resuming a game of I Spy, which included "something green and slimy," "a very old person" and "an *Englischer* wearing a funny hat."

Nick directed his mare into Howie's parking area,

which was really just a grassy spot under some trees, and the boys shot out of the buggy, greeting their grandparents as if they hadn't seen them in years. Simon pulled his buggy in right after theirs. In a blink, Christopher had joined the boys, Simon began talking to Nick about summer crops, and Mary joined Deborah at the back of the group.

"You and Nick were looking quite snuggly."

"Snuggly?"

"Well, you were standing close."

"Because he helped me out of the buggy—that's all. There's nothing to it."

Mary wiggled her eyebrows. "Didn't know you needed help out of a buggy these days." Then she slipped her arm through the crook of Deborah's and guided her toward the group.

They stood in a line in front of the small trailer that was Howie's Ice Cream, studying the board of flavors. Deborah glanced at Nick, thinking of the strange way he'd acted when they'd gone kayaking, of the ice cream he'd bought her, of the way he'd held her hand.

He hadn't done anything like that since.

She supposed he was simply trying to give the impression that they were really dating to the others. Somehow, at the time, it had felt different, but perhaps she'd made that up. Her feelings regarding Nick were quite confused. She was getting what she deserved for coming up with a dating scheme to start with. She should have simply told her parents the truth—that she wasn't ready to date.

But she'd tried that.

And in a moment of weakness, she'd agreed that she would date by that summer. It was Nick or the list of widowers her mother had compiled.

Nick slipped back beside her, lowered his voice and asked, "Having a hard time deciding?"

"Yes, something like that." And then she started laughing, because he had no idea that she was referring to men and not flavors of ice cream.

She supposed there was a comparison there, though. You might enjoy a scoop of pistachio, but did you want it for the rest of your life? Probably not. At the same time, vanilla would be rather boring if that was all you could have. She stepped up to the window, ordered a double dip of chocolate chip and strawberry, and smiled back at Nick. Strawberry reminded her of Jacob and Joseph and their red hair. And chocolate chip? Well, it seemed to perfectly represent this man who could make her angry or make her laugh—often at the same time.

Ten minutes later they were gathered around the picnic table.

"I love birthdays," Joseph confessed.

"I love ice cream." Jacob managed to get a spot of chocolate on his nose and then couldn't figure out what everyone was laughing about.

When it came time to give the boys their gifts, Deborah felt somewhat self-conscious. On the one hand, they both needed new hats, but on the other hand, it seemed rather boring.

Jacob and Joseph were thrilled. Both hats were straw with a black band. She'd marked their initials on the inside, though she suspected Joseph's would stay pristine much longer than Jacob's.

"Use your old hat when you're working at Nick's," she reminded them.

"*Ya.* That way if I slip in the hog pen again, my hat won't get dirty."

She closed her eyes and tried not to envision that scene.

Her parents gave the boys a new deck of Dutch Blitz cards and a new checkers set. Their old set was missing several pieces, and they'd taken to using buttons for markers.

Simon, Mary and Christopher gave them small coolers for carrying their lunch to school—red for Jacob and blue for Joseph.

But it was the gift from Nick that brought tears to Deborah's eyes.

Jacob received a new baseball mitt. Joseph's gift was a book on raising animals—written on a level he could understand and with plenty of pictures. What pierced Deborah's heart was how well Nick knew her boys. Jacob would rather play catch than any other thing she could think of. He was constantly throwing the ball for Blue, and on Sundays the baseball game after church was the highlight of his weekend.

Joseph did those things with his *bruder*, but he was fascinated by animals—their mares, Nick's pigs and goats, even Nick's dog. He had more questions than Deborah had answers, and often her *dat* was already retired for the evening.

Nick had understood what both boys would treasure most.

She mouthed *"danki,"* and Nick nodded in response.

Jacob declared it the best birthday ever, and Joseph beamed at everyone and thanked them again and again.

Simon, Mary and Christopher said they needed to get home—their move day was coming faster than anyone was ready to accept.

It was her *mamm*'s idea that the boys ride home with them, declaring they were lonely in the big old buggy all by themselves. Then she winked at Deborah, causing her to wish that the ground would swallow her there and then.

She should have enjoyed the ride home alone with Nick. Mothers had precious few moments that were quiet and undisturbed, but her heart felt tender—sore, almost. It was a familiar feeling, one that sometimes threatened to overwhelm her.

"It was a *gut* day, *ya*?" Nick waited for her answer, glancing her way and then back toward the road. "What's wrong?"

"Nothing, I guess." She sighed. "They're growing up so fast."

"Oh, *ya*. Seven to seventeen will happen quick." He snapped his fingers so she could fully understand what quick meant. Growing serious, he said, "Let me guess—baby blues."

Now she did laugh. "What do you know about baby blues?"

"Lydia goes through it when every baby learns to walk. It's as if she's lost something once they're able to ambulate on their own."

"Ambulate?"

"To walk from place to place."

"I know what it means." She shook her head but appreciated his effort to lighten her mood. "It could be that, I suppose. Most Amish *kinner* have a baby *schweschder* or *bruder* by the time they're seven."

"Most have several."

"That's my point." Now she angled in the seat so that she could study him. "Jacob and Joseph aren't living a normal Amish life."

"Because you haven't had another baby?"

"And they don't have a father." The words popped out of her mouth before she could stop them.

Nick didn't answer immediately. He didn't brush away her concerns or assure her that she was making mountains out of molehills. "I think we want to believe that everyone in an Amish community has the same life, but it's not true."

"What do you mean?"

"Everyone doesn't have the perfect family."

"I never said they did."

"Take Lydia, for example, my *schweschder*-in-law. Her *dat* died right after she was born, and her *mamm* didn't remarry for many years. She grew up thinking of her older *bruders* as her father figure."

"Okay."

Now he grinned. "She turned out just fine. Jacob and Joseph will turn out just fine, too."

"But how do you know that?"

"I think the Scripture tells us as much."

"It does?"

"I can't say as I know all of the Bible, but I know enough of it to understand the basics."

"Such as?"

"*Gotte* has a plan for each of us, and He loves us."

"I guess."

"Nope—you know I'm right. You just don't want to admit it." He reached over and tugged on one of her *kapp* strings, and she slapped his hand away.

They both laughed at the absurdity of it—acting like *kinner* when they were grown adults. Next, he'd be sneaking a frog into her school desk.

As they pulled into her parents' place, Deborah found herself wishing the drive had lasted longer. She hadn't realized until that very moment how much her talks with Nick helped. She needed someone her age to share her worries and emotions and dreams with each day.

She shouldn't get used to Nick, though. She shouldn't depend on him. They'd stop their fake relationship by the end of the summer, he'd find a nice girl to settle down with and Deborah would once again be on her own.

He set the brake on the buggy, hopped out and was at her door when she opened it. He reached for her hand, helped her down, then intertwined his fingers with hers. How could such a simple thing calm her so? They walked slowly, shoulder to shoulder, covering the space from the buggy to the front porch all too quickly.

Their relationship most certainly was make-believe. She reminded herself of that fact often, but maybe she could pretend that it was real for a little longer.

July passed in a rush of days spent tending goats, pigs, crops and two energetic boys.

Nick thought it might be the best summer of his life, other than his tendency to wrestle over his relationship with Deborah—or rather, his lack of a relationship. The plan he'd had to introduce her to one of the men at the kayaking trip hadn't panned out. He had no doubt one or two might be interested. He'd even met up with two of the guys once to go fishing, but he'd lost his nerve at the last second. He didn't want to give them the number for the phone shack closest to Deborah. He didn't want them to even think that she was available.

He wasn't the right man for Deborah, but who was?

Nick tried to put it out of his mind, which was impossible to do. Especially since they continued to go out on a "date" once a week. It didn't help that he'd invariably hold her hand or touch her shoulder or sit closer than was strictly necessary. It was as if his mind understood the absurdity of it. He wasn't ready to court anyone, and he knew it. But his heart? That was proving a bit harder to convince.

Instead of attempting to deal with the situation, he worked longer hours, checked out more library books to read up on farming and goats and pigs, even planted an extra field that he hadn't planned on cultivating until the following year—anything to keep busy and help him fall asleep at night.

The one bright spot of the summer was Deborah's twins.

The boys continued to create nearly as much work as they completed, but somehow it bothered Nick less. There was a lot to do to help the pigs settle in—a pigpen to build and fencing to put up. They'd done that the first week. Giving the animal book to Joseph might not have been a good idea.

"They need a mud wallow, Nick. I read about it again last night. I can show you the page, if you'd like."

"Yes! I am all about making mud." Jacob dropped the brush he'd been using to care for the goats. One look from Nick, and he picked it back up. "I'll just go put this on the shelf in the barn."

"*Gut* idea."

By the time he was back, Joseph had convinced Nick that a mud wallow was indeed a good and necessary thing for pigs. According to the book, it would help the pigs keep their body temperature down and also served to promote good skin condition. Nick wasn't one to argue with the written word, so they set about creating a mud bath positioned across the end of the pig enclosure.

This required that he dig down two feet and line the bottom with bricks. Fortunately, there was a big stack of old bricks behind the barn. Jacob and Joseph loaded them in the wheelbarrow, pushed it to the pigpen and then helped him to place them along the bottom of the enclosure. Next, they put the soil he'd dug out back in and added some red soil, which had to be carted from the west field. The boys returned wearing nearly as much dirt as they'd managed to put in the wheelbarrow. Their clothes were almost as red as their hair.

"Where will we get the water?" Joseph asked.

Jacob hopped from one foot to the other. "Carting it over here in a bucket will be a lot of extra work every day."

Nick sat back on his heels, scanning his farm. Snapping his fingers, he said, "There's an old lawn hose in the barn, next to the feed sacks."

The boys took off without being asked.

"They certainly save me some steps," Nick muttered to himself—or he thought he was talking to himself until Deborah responded.

"You might gain weight if the boys do all of your fetching." She stepped up on the bottom board of the fence, draped her arms over the top and smiled down at him.

He was suddenly aware of how sweaty, dirty and grimy he was. "When did you get here?"

"Just now. Building a pig wallow?"

"What was your first clue?"

"My son read those pages to us at breakfast. I sort of figured he might talk you into it."

"Joseph can be persuasive, and Jacob is always so eager to run anywhere." He stood and stretched, popping his back and feeling every day of his thirty-five years. He might have let out a small groan to go with the popping.

Deborah's eyebrows arched and she started laughing, but she didn't have time to tease him. The boys arrived with the hose, Nick connected it to the faucet next to the horse trough and Deborah held the end—pointed toward the new mud-and-brick enclosure.

"How did that three little pigs story go?" Joseph asked.

"The first pig made his house of straw." Jacob shook his head, as if he couldn't fathom such silliness. He pulled off his hat and scratched his head. "And the second—"

"The second built his house of sticks." Deborah was now directing a steady drip of water toward the mud.

The sow and piglets Nick had purchased stood at the far end, grunting and studying them but not moving any closer.

"The old wolf blew down both houses, if I remember correctly." Nick had climbed out of the pen, and now he stood next to Deborah, his shoulder touching hers. She glanced at him and then away, as if suddenly quite interested in her job of creating mud.

"But the third pig's house was made of bricks," Jacob said, laughing. "The wolf couldn't blow it down."

"Maybe that's why we make mud wallows out of bricks." Joseph jogged over to where the pigs were huddled in the corner of their pen.

Nick lowered his voice so that only Deborah could hear him. "Joseph has a way with those animals. Watch this."

As she watched, he dropped to his knees and scratched the large sow behind the ears. The piglets, who at first were huddled behind the sow, poked their heads out and were soon nuzzling around Joseph.

Jacob was sitting on the opposite side of the fence. "Come on, Momma Pig. Show those babies what to do."

It didn't take a lot of encouragement.

Joseph walked toward the mud wallow. The sow followed Joseph, and the piglets followed the sow. She sniffed suspiciously at the mud, then squealed and flopped over, rubbing her back against the muddy bricks, feet in the air, a contented look on her face—if a pig could have a contented look. The piglets crowded in beside her. She flopped back over to her stomach, snout down, and let out a contented *oink*.

Jacob and Joseph high-fived one another.

Deborah laughed and proclaimed them to be "*gut* pigs."

They spent the next fifteen minutes putting away tools. Nick suspected that Deborah hadn't come over just to see him. No doubt she was ready for the boys to return home. They often stayed past lunch and into the afternoon. Most days, Nick found himself taking on a project that had not been on his weekly to-do list. Usually it was something—like the mud wallow—that he thought the boys would enjoy.

He probably needed to focus more on his list.

Deborah walked over to the goats, cooing and calling to the younger ones. Jacob and Joseph dashed back and forth in a game of impromptu tag.

Soon the boys would be in school all day, Deborah would be at her parents' place or her job, and then he could resume following his schedule. He told himself that he'd be mighty glad when that happened, but a small part of him wondered if he'd get lonely.

He glanced at Deborah again and wondered what it would be like to kiss her.

Would he be lonely when they were all busy with their own lives?

He'd purposely purchased his own farm a few miles from his *bruder* so that he'd have plenty of time alone. He enjoyed the solitary life. Family was *gut*, and of course he liked spending time with his nieces and nephew, but he thought of himself as what the *Englisch* would call an introvert. *Ha.* Put a picture of an Amish farmer beside the definition of introvert. It would be spot-on.

Deborah was still calling out to the goats, leaning over the top of the fence and trying to tempt them with a carrot. Jacob and Joseph were standing next to the pump, trying to swipe the dirt off their pants, which only succeeded in spreading it around.

"Boys, there are food scraps in the bucket under my sink. Want to fetch them for me?"

He was rather surprised that they hadn't fallen in the mud, or flung it at one another, or even traipsed it into his house. Of course, it was the first day with the wallow. He suspected they'd manage all those things before the end of the week.

He waited until they were out of sight, and then Nick did what he'd wanted to do since he'd looked up from the mud and seen Deborah staring down at him.

He made his way over to the goat fence, careful not to make too much noise, and stopped when his shoulder was brushing up against Deborah's. She pulled back in surprise, but he shook his head—once, definitively. She studied him, the look on her face one of curiosity and uncertainty. He didn't wait. He didn't weigh the pros and cons. He gently turned her shoulders so that she was facing him, leaned forward, and he kissed her—at first lightly, then again, properly this time. Thoroughly.

Her cheeks turned a rosy pink, and he figured that he'd done the thing correctly, though he was no expert at kissing. It had been a while. Still, he supposed some things you didn't forget. The boys clambered out of his house, carrying the scraps bucket and singing a made-up song about pigs.

In that moment, Nick thought that everything was right with his world. It was as it should be. And the look on Deborah's face gave him hope that she felt the same.

Seeing the boys, she turned toward them, straightened the apron over her dress and checked her *kapp*.

"You look perfect," he said in a low voice, which caused her to blush even more dramatically.

She began walking toward her parents' farm, then turned and walked backward. "Dinner in thirty minutes, boys." And without another word, she practically sprinted back home.

He'd rattled her.

Why had he done that?

Why had he kissed her?

He'd just had a conversation with himself about how satisfied he was being alone.

But he'd definitely flustered her, and that was fine by him, because it meant that she felt as confused and lovelorn as he did. At least, he thought that was what it meant.

The next question was, what was he going to do about it?

Perhaps it was time to ask her.

Maybe it was time to end this fake dating and begin their relationship in earnest.

Yes, it was the opposite of what he'd decided not

twenty minutes earlier. Good grief, he was a mess. Possibly it was time to get some advice, and he knew just the person he should speak to.

Chapter Nine

Deborah felt as if she spent the next few weeks in something of a dream state. Whole days seemed to pass without her being aware of them. She was actually surprised when her *mamm* changed the wall calendar to August.

How could it already be August?

What had happened to the summer?

Everything was going well—perhaps too well. She felt as if she was waiting for the other shoe to drop.

Jacob and Joseph were thriving. They clearly loved their time spent with Nick, and Deborah couldn't remember the last time Nick had complained about the boys. They still managed to find trouble when they were at home. Like the time they were going to help her pick the produce from the family garden, and they ended up finding a garden snake, which they then sneaked into their bedroom. Deborah found it and nearly had a heart attack when she was picking up their dirty laundry— something Nick would probably insist they should do themselves.

They *should* do it themselves.

But each step of independence and maturity was a

step away from her, and it already felt as if her heart was breaking.

Maybe she did have baby blues.

It didn't help that her emotions regarding Nick were all over the place. Her parents were plainly hopeful that they'd be making an announcement soon. Deborah felt terrible about that. She was going to have to correct their assumptions eventually—and sooner rather than later, or they'd be planning her wedding.

She and Nick had continued to go on a date once a week. But he hadn't kissed her again. In fact, he'd pulled away. Why had he pulled away? Had she done something wrong? Had he realized that a ready-made family was more than he cared to take on? Had she misread the whole thing? Was their relationship fake, or was it real?

The one bright spot was that her job was going well, and she was finally overcoming her guilt about enjoying it. She was *gut* with yarn, had even created several original patterns, and now she was teaching a class at the yarn shop. They'd had to cap the attendance at a dozen because that was all the chairs they could rustle up. She loved that group of women. Loved being with them, hearing their laughter and watching their skill grow. The group was comprised of Amish and *Englisch*, young and old. What they shared was a love for knitting, for creating something both beautiful and useful for their family members.

Working at the yarn shop had opened Deborah up to the person she'd been before her life had gone off track. And perhaps it had shown her that having her own dreams and being a *gut mamm* were both possible.

But, oh, how she mourned the way summer seemed to fly.

Her two little boys would be going to school. They'd

become older boys, then young men. They weren't her babies anymore.

Finally, the day for the school cleaning arrived. Deborah had been dreading it, though the boys had written it on the calendar and even circled it with a blue crayon.

Saturday, August 27, was a fine summer day. The terrible heat of the week before had eased, and a light north wind stirred the leaves on the trees. Deborah's *mamm* said she'd be along later. The older women tended to put out a lunch spread while the parents of the schoolchildren worked to ready the single classroom, bathrooms and playground.

She was surprised when she drove up to the little one-room schoolhouse and saw so many buggies. There were nearly a dozen, and she very quickly picked out Nick's.

Nick?

Why was Nick here?

She supposed it wasn't so unusual for him to come. Sometimes bachelors did lend a hand, or so she told herself as the boys jogged off to join their friends, who were painting the long board fence that surrounded the schoolyard.

"Good thing you put them in their old clothes."

She nearly jumped out of her apron, spinning around to find Nick standing right behind her. "I noticed your buggy," she murmured, trying to look anywhere but directly at him. Why did her heart race so when he stood next to her? Maybe she was coming down with something. Or maybe she had a crush on Nicholas Stoltzfus. She was definitely acting like a lovesick schoolgirl.

"My buggy looks like all the others."

"All right. I suppose I noticed Big Girl, then."

"Sure you weren't looking for me?"

Her face felt suddenly hot, but she ignored the insinuation and walked toward the schoolhouse. "Since you have no children, I was surprised. That's all."

"Oh, I heard that they could use an extra hand. Turns out the roof needs a bit of repair."

It was then that she noticed the ladders and the men hoisting up shingles to other men, who were standing on the schoolhouse roof.

"Want to come up and help us?"

"I do not."

"It's a beautiful view up there."

Why was he intent on teasing her? She hurried up the porch steps, flung a "be careful and don't fall off" over her shoulder, and escaped into the single large room.

Women were already cleaning chalkboards, washing windows and moving desks. Deborah spent the next two hours scrubbing floors and using soapy water on cubbies. The teacher was the same they'd had the year before, though of course Deborah hadn't formally met her.

The woman's name was Nancy. She was a Mennonite who lived in Shipshewana proper, and she had a husband and four grown children of her own. She was short with gray hair that was covered with a traditional Mennonite veiling. She wore a long dress and smiled readily, which did much to set Deborah's mind at ease.

Nancy offered a greeting and thank-you to the group as they settled down for lunch.

"I hope that if you have any concerns, you will come and speak to me about them. No need to lie awake worrying over a thing. Also, those of you who had me last year know that I like to send notes home in lunch boxes, so look for at least one note a week from me. It doesn't mean your little one is in trouble, only that I like to keep you up-to-date."

The boys and girls collectively dropped their heads into their hands, which caused laughter to spread around the table.

"For my new moms and dads, I want you to rest easy. Your children will learn, not only from me, but also from the older children in the schoolhouse. We have a fine group of scholars here, and I'm proud to be their teacher."

Deborah sincerely hoped that the teacher still felt that way after trying to corral Jacob and Joseph into a desk every school day. Nancy sat down at an adjacent table, Bishop Ezekiel offered a blessing over the meal and the school year, and conversations around each table resumed. Deborah tried to pay attention, but her thoughts were all over the place.

She must have eaten her lunch, because she looked down and the plate was empty. She didn't even remember chewing. Smiling at the women sitting next to her, she stood and excused herself. Perhaps she needed a little comfort food. Sugar surely would help her mood, which was plummeting faster than the thermometer after the first cold front.

Nick sidled up beside her at the dessert table as she was trying to decide between a brownie and a piece of pie. "Take one of each. You look worried."

"I am worried."

Nick leaned closer and lowered his voice. "She seems perfectly capable to me. No doubt she's dealt with twins before."

"Yes, but we're talking about Jacob and Joseph. Jacob tried building a frog house in the mudroom last week—without telling me—so when I fetched the bucket and mop, several frogs jumped out at once, and then off they went, hopping through the house."

"Didn't she say she's been teaching for twenty years? Certainly those classes included plenty of energetic young boys."

"Maybe." She turned to study him and thought back to that first day when she'd met him. She'd thought that he looked tall, handsome and overly serious. He still looked tall and handsome, but now she understood that his seriousness was a shell he wore to keep people at arm's length. When he relaxed, he laughed and teased and his eyes squinted in a way that made her want to slide her fingers from his temple to his jawline.

She grabbed the pie and turned away from him, heading toward the playground so that she could put some space between them. Nick didn't take the hint. He picked up two brownies and followed her to the swings.

Plopping down in one, she stabbed her fork into the lemon meringue and put a nice-sized bite into her mouth.

Sweet, tart, creamy.

That should fix any mood.

Nick dropped into the swing beside her and was making a swipe for the rest of her lemon pie when someone called his name from across the playground.

"Are you ready?" Stephen Lapp called.

"Sure. *Ya.* Coming." But before he left, he leaned closer to Deborah. "You owe me a bite of pie."

"I do not. Get your own."

"What fun would that be?" And with a wink he was gone, jogging to catch up with Stephen.

"They're going to get firewood," Anna explained, taking the swing that Nick had been occupying.

Anna had been in the same grade as Deborah. They'd been friends long ago, but they'd grown apart once they were both out of school. Deborah had left to live with her *aenti* in Sugarcreek, had met Gavin, fallen in love and found herself pregnant. She realized that was a watershed moment in her life. Not the move or Gavin or even finding herself handling the situation alone. No, deciding to have her boys had been the moment in her life that separated all others. There was before the boys and after the boys. It seemed that her life had become what it was destined to be on the day they were born.

Now, watching them play a game of baseball with the older kids, her eyes stung with tears. She'd been so busy focusing on getting through each day that she hadn't appreciated how quickly time with them would pass.

"My *schweschder* tells me it's normal to feel emotional when our oldest starts school. Seems I was just bringing Suzie home from the birthing center, and now she's playing school at the kitchen table—practicing, as she calls it. I've been blubbering all week."

"I thought I'd be happy to have a few hours to myself. Now I have no idea what I'll do with all that time." Deborah smiled and swiped at her eyes.

Anna laughed and switched her baby boy from her left shoulder to her right. "Baby Aaron and the four in between keep me plenty busy, but it's still a bittersweet moment."

"Aaron is beautiful." Deborah would have asked to hold him, but she didn't think her heart could handle any more ache at the moment. "How old is he?"

"Three months and still not sleeping all night. All of my others did, but Aaron here is intent on being a stinker." She held him up, kissed his forehead, then settled him across her knees. "Your boys seem to have grown quite fond of Nick."

Deborah's mind went blank. How was she supposed to answer that?

"Which must be...you know, a weight off your mind."

"Because..."

"Because you two are dating."

Deborah looked at her, wide-eyed and waiting.

What was she waiting for?

Anna lowered her voice. "He seems quite smitten with you."

"Nick?" The word came out two octaves higher than she intended. "Oh, I don't know about that."

"Sometimes it's hard to see when you're in the middle of a thing." Aaron started fussing, and Anna stood, jostling him over her left shoulder. "I best go and feed him, but if you need any help, you know, with plans..."

"Plans?"

"Wedding plans, silly. If you need help, let me know." And then she was gone, walking toward the schoolhouse, where she could nurse the baby. As for Aaron, he stared over his *mamm*'s shoulder at Deborah, then shoved his thumb into his mouth. Life was apparently pretty simple if you were three months old.

Wedding plans...

Deborah glanced around the group that was now breaking up to finish the last few chores. Were they expecting her and Nick to announce their intention to marry? What had she been thinking? How had she let this fake dating get out of hand?

Nick had no intention of marrying her. He had a five-year plan. She'd seen it, and her name was nowhere on the list.

She stood and brushed off her skirt, then marched back into the schoolhouse. The floor under the teacher's desk could use a good scrubbing, and Deborah had enough frustration to tackle the project enthusiastically.

But somehow, it didn't stop Anna's words from echoing in her mind. *If you need help, let me know.*

Nick had told himself he'd be thrilled to have his mornings to himself, but the first day of school seemed to crawl at a snail's pace. He finished twice as much as he would have with the boys there. Not that it improved his mood.

By the time he sat down to eat lunch on the front porch—a lunch that he ate alone, because the boys were at school—he admitted to himself that he'd become used to having Jacob and Joseph around. Jacob was barely able to sit through lunch, often bouncing up to tell a story, using both of his hands and hopping around for effect. Joseph always shared at least one tidbit he'd recently read about pigs or goats or sheep.

Are you sure you don't want sheep, Nick? My book says they're gut animals to raise.

Sheep were not in his business plan.

Neither were two little boys, but they'd managed to wriggle their way into his heart.

Their beautiful mother was not someone he should be preoccupied with, but how could he help it? He had wanted to kiss her while she was sitting on the swing. He'd wanted to hold her hand and walk her to her buggy. He wanted everyone to know how he felt about Deborah Mast. He'd spoken to his *bruder*, who had told him to *plant something or get out of the field.* He was pretty sure David had made that up. It certainly wasn't a proverb he'd ever heard before.

By the time three o'clock rolled around, he'd decided he really needed to cut the grass out by the mailbox. "Want to go with me, boy?" Blue grabbed his favorite ball and trotted down the lane in front of him. Nick wasn't too surprised that Deborah was already there, arms crossed, foot tapping, watching for Jacob and Joseph.

"Wouldn't let you pick them up, huh?"

"Nope. Insisted they could walk to and from school alone, just like any other young scholar." She worried her thumbnail.

"Sounds like something Joseph would have said."

Blue dropped to the ground, his ball beside him, his head on his paws, watching in the same direction they were. Did the dog actually know where the boys had gone and that they were both standing there waiting for their return? Could a dog sense that?

"How did getting them off to school this morning go?"

"Jacob simply ducked away from my kiss and headed out the door. Joseph paused long enough to give me a two-second hug." She turned toward him and cocked her head. "Wait a minute. What are you doing here?"

"Me? I'm just cutting grass around this mailbox." He dropped to his knees and began using the hand cutters that he'd had to go back and grab because he'd forgotten them the first time he'd started down the lane.

Deborah propped her elbows on the mailbox and gave him a quizzical look. "You want me to believe you just happened to be out here working?"

"Part of being a farmer. Our work is never done." He sighed heavily. "Plus, I just lost my two best workers, so there's more for me to do."

"And that's why trimming grass around the mailbox rose to the top of your list?"

Before he could answer, they heard laughter, and both turned in the direction of the schoolhouse. Jacob and Joseph were walking down the middle of the road, apparently kicking a rock all the way home. Blue sent a beseeching look to Nick.

"Sure, go ahead."

Which was all the permission the dog needed. Jacob and Joseph broke into a run when they spied Blue. Both boys exclaimed over him as if they hadn't seen him in weeks. When they looked up and saw Deborah and Nick, they again broke into a sprint.

Nick had thought they might be tired after a full day of school, but apparently that wasn't the case. They had as much energy as usual, possibly more.

"How was school?" Deborah asked even before they'd arrived.

"Gut." Both boys skidded to a stop.

"Our teacher has an entire shelf of books, *Mamm*." Joseph smiled broadly. "We can check one out each weekend."

Jacob dropped his lunch box down on the ground and opened it. "We're supposed to call her Nancy. Boy, she can really give you the *be still* look."

"Yup. Even Jacob was still when she did that."

"Everyone was."

"We got to sit by each other."

"And the older boys let us play baseball at lunch."

Jacob pulled out a single sheet of paper and thrust it in her hands. "Our first assignment was about our family. Look, I got a star. See that, Nick? A star, right there by my name."

Nick glanced over Deborah's shoulder, saw Jacob's name and the gold star. The drawing was of a stick family whose heads were extraordinarily large compared to the rest of their bodies.

"I got a star, too." Joseph pulled his sheet from his

pocket and carefully unfolded it. "We could write or draw, so I decided to write."

"And I decided to draw."

Nick looked from the drawing to the page of writing. Both were titled *My Family*. Deborah had gone suddenly still. Her eyes widened, and he detected a sharp intake of breath. He looked at the drawing closer. "Hey. You included Blue."

Jacob's page was filled—left to right—with stick figures. Each figure had round eyes and a huge smile. Bethany and John, Deborah, Jacob, Joseph and Nick. They stood between a tree and a pond with their stick-figure hands connected to one another. The adults were nearly as tall as the tree, which, if Nick wasn't mistaken, was the maple tree by the pond at the back of John's property. A stick dog, colored blue, stuck his head out between the two boys.

Nick reached out to read what Joseph had written, but Deborah snatched the papers away, folded them neatly and handed them back to the boys. "Go show these to *Mammi*. She'll want to put them in the home-work box, and I think she has cookies and milk ready for you both."

That was all Jacob and Joseph needed to hear. Giving Blue one last pat, their mother a hug and Nick a high five, they raced toward the house.

It was nice to have the boys home, and Nick was pleased they'd had a *gut* first day. He didn't realize that he'd been worried about that. It was important to enjoy your schoolmates, your teacher and the entire school environment. Otherwise, it would be a long year for everyone. Perhaps Deborah could stop worrying now. Perhaps he could stop worrying.

"See? There was nothing to be concerned about. They both had a *wunderbaar* day."

"We need to talk."

"Talk?"

"About us." Her arms were crossed tightly around her middle—as if she had a stomachache—and her lips formed a straight line.

He glanced around in surprise. Something had changed in the last few minutes, but he had no idea what it was. "I'm not…" He swallowed and then tried again. "I'm not sure what you're referring to, exactly."

Deborah raised her chin a fraction of an inch, but she didn't quite meet his eyes. Instead, she stared at a spot over his right shoulder, then down at the dog, then back at her house.

"Of course you don't know what I'm talking about. This has all been some sort of game to you."

"This—"

"Our dating."

"Wait a minute, Deborah. That was your idea."

"I know it was. I came up with this ridiculous plan, and so I suppose it's my job to end it."

"End it?"

"Our fake dating." Now she looked directly at him, and Nick had a sudden moment of clarity that he was messing this up. What was he supposed to do? What should he say? He was suddenly aware that Deborah was fighting to show an expression of disinterest, but underneath, he sensed that she was feeling vulnerable.

"About that…" He reached for her hand, but she snatched it away. "What I was about to say was that it wasn't fake for me."

"It must have been. It was for both of us." She forced a smile.

"Don't say that." His voice was low now. He didn't fully understand what was happening, but he didn't like the direction this conversation was going. "Deborah, I care about you."

"*Nein*, you don't."

"Why would you say that?" Now his temper was piercing his confusion.

"You've never misled me, Nick." She dropped her arms and stood even straighter. "You've never once said you had feelings for me, so don't expect me to believe you do now."

"I know I haven't *said* it, but—"

"And people are talking." The pretense fell away, and the confusion, fear and sadness in her expression caused an actual ache in his heart. "People at church, at the school, probably even my parents. And my boys?"

She stared toward her house, then again crossed her arms as if she needed to protect herself, as if she needed to guard her heart. "Jacob is drawing you in his family picture, and Joseph is writing about you. I won't have it. I will not have them getting their hopes up. I won't have them thinking that something is real when it isn't."

"But—"

"Unless I'm wrong. Unless you do care for us, all three of us…"

He hesitated, because he knew this was an important moment. He wanted to get it right.

Unfortunately, Deborah took his hesitation to mean something else entirely. "You were correct when you said this was my idea, and now it's time for me to do the right thing and be honest with those I love."

And with those words, she strode away, leaving him standing by the mailbox, grass cutters in his hand, Blue at his side and a world of questions and regrets weighing him down.

Chapter Ten

Deborah was tempted to stick with her original plan—tell her parents that she and Nick had tried dating, but things hadn't worked. They were simply too different. She could probably tell that story convincingly, since it seemed they were too different. In the end, she couldn't go through with the lie. They deserved to know the truth.

After dinner that evening, while the boys were upstairs getting ready for bed, she told her *mamm* and *dat* everything. She explained about her idea to fake date Nick, how they'd become friends but nothing more, and that now she was worried Jacob and Joseph were becoming attached to Nick. She was sorry that she'd tried to deceive them, all because she was embarrassed. She'd chosen to be less than honest rather than have the difficult conversation that she knew was coming.

"We've had this conversation about your dating before." Her *dat* seemed to be choosing his words carefully. "Our reason for wanting you to... It's not because we don't want you here."

He paused, waited, made certain he had her complete attention. When Deborah nodded, he continued.

"Having Jacob and Joseph around, having you home again, has been one of the greatest blessings of my older years. But what I want isn't enough in this case. You deserve more, Deborah. And those boys deserve a *dat*, should *Gotte* have one for them."

"Which you can't know unless you actually come out of your shell." Her *mamm* reached for her hand, then, upon seeing her tears, she turned to snag the box of Kleenex and pushed it into Deborah's lap. "I understand that you were hurt before, that Gavin did not cherish and honor you as you should be. That's his loss, Deborah."

"But I made..." She hiccupped and pressed the Kleenex to her eyes. Why were her tears like water from a faucet? Would the day never come when she'd cried herself dry? "I made that mistake. My boys shouldn't have to pay for it."

"Your boys are lucky to have you as their *mamm*. You're a *gut mamm*, Deborah." Her *dat* waited until she looked up. "Your *mamm* and I have prayed over this many a night. We want you to have a complete family. We want you to know the kind of love that we share."

"But what if I never do? What if that isn't in *Gotte*'s plan for me?"

"He gives *gut* things to His children, but let's for a moment say you're right. Let's consider that possibly *Gotte* intends for you to raise those two boys upstairs by yourself." At that exact moment, there was a thud from above, followed by boyish laughter. Her *dat* smiled and reached out to pat her hand. "Then you will do that, and your family and neighbors and church will help you. But how can you know such a thing for certain if you don't at least open up your heart to the possibility of love?"

"We're happy to have you here with us, Deborah. We would be happy for you to stay for the rest of our days." Her *mamm* shook her head and sat back on the couch. "But that's a selfish thing on our part when it's possible that you could have a husband, a home of your own and more *kinner.* To think that you would miss out on all of that because you're comfortable here, because you're hurt or shy or afraid…"

"That's not what we want."

Deborah nodded and pulled in a deep breath. "You're right. You're both right. At first, I think it was because I was still hurting from Gavin's rejection…"

"Eight years ago, Deborah…or very nearly eight."

"Right." She sat up straighter, smoothed out the fabric of her dress. "After that, I guess it was just easier to live here and believe no one wanted me. Much easier than putting my heart on the line, or my boys…"

She thought of Nick, thought of the boys' *My Family* assignment and fought to swallow more tears. But she was tired of crying. She was tired of being afraid.

"Your boys will mirror your attitude. If you're heart-broken and bitter and afraid, they will be, too." Her *dat* tapped the arm of his rocker. "I know you don't want that for them. Show them how to be courageous, how to love courageously. Be the type of person that you hope they will grow into."

"I'll try." She closed her eyes, then opened them and looked around the room. This house—the place she'd grown up in, the place she'd fled to when life became too much to handle alone—it had been a true haven of peace for her. Had she become too content here? Was she too eager to pretend this was her only option? What happened to the young girl who envisioned her own home, a loving husband, a roomful of *kinner*? When had she given up on her own dreams?

"I'll try," she repeated. "*Mamm*, let's get out your bachelor list tomorrow and decide how to proceed."

"We'll start with the younger men. I know all too well how you feel about older widowers." Everyone laughed, though even that felt as if it hurt Deborah's heart.

She'd thought the conversation with her parents would be the worst part of the night, but as she made her way upstairs, she knew that she owed it to her boys to be honest with them as well.

She explained to them that she'd made a mistake, that she and Nick were only friends, that they wouldn't be going on dates any longer.

Jacob was lying on his bed, tossing a tennis ball against the ceiling. "Does this mean we can't go over to see Nick anymore?"

"Of course not. He'll still be our friend and our neighbor." She hoped that was true. She wasn't particularly proud of how she'd treated him earlier that day.

"Works for me."

Joseph was sitting up on the side of his bed, a closed book in his lap. "So, you're saying that he won't be our *dat*."

"I'm sorry, honey, but *nein*—I don't think so."

"You don't think so, which means he could be."

The hope in that last statement caused tears to sting Deborah's eyes, but she blinked them away. "I'm going to quit pretending I know the answers or what the future holds, but I wouldn't get your hopes up about that."

Joseph finally looked up at her, and the vulnerability she saw on his face pierced her heart. "Did we do something wrong?"

"You most certainly did not. It's just marriage requires a stronger bond than friendship. Nick and I are friends, but nothing more."

Even as she uttered those words, she wondered if she was lying again, so she added, "At least I don't think we are."

Both boys hugged her, assured her that they were a *gut* family, just the three of them, and Jacob offered to erase Nick from his picture.

"*Nein.* One day we'll all laugh about that, so let's not erase him."

"*Gut.* It would have left a big hole." He resumed tossing his ball at the ceiling.

"Time for bed. You are scholars now, and you have school tomorrow."

That reminder earned her some groans, but both boys were smiling as she bent to kiss them. They didn't even plead for five more minutes when she turned out the battery-powered table lamp. No doubt they were as exhausted from the day as she was.

She was at the door when Joseph called her back. "Nick sure seemed to like you. I guess you could be wrong about how he feels. Right?"

"I could be, but I don't think so."

"Good night, *Mamm.*"

"Good night, Joseph."

"'Night, *Mamm.*"

"Good night, Jacob."

She realized as she went to her room that they hadn't talked about how she felt about Nick. She wasn't even sure. As she prepared for bed, she forced herself to look directly at that question.

Did she care for him?

Did she love him?

She might. It could be that he'd worked his way under

her protective shell. Or perhaps seeing him with her boys, seeing him teaching and caring for them, had caused her to drop her guard.

But she had asked him, point-blank, if he cared for her in that way. He'd stood there stumbling over his words and glancing around for the nearest exit.

She sighed, pulled back her quilt and slipped between the sheets. She shouldn't have been so upset with him, and she'd need to apologize for that. After all, it wasn't his fault that her boys had included him in the family drawing and essay.

Nick wasn't to blame, but she'd done the right thing. She was done with fake dating, with pretense and artifice. It was time to start living her life authentically. Even if it meant that, once again, she had to start over alone. She wasn't really alone, though. There were plenty of people who loved her—the two boys down the hall, her parents downstairs, her siblings and even her friends. Perhaps one day she would laugh with Anna about this. She definitely did not need help planning a wedding.

But perhaps one day she would.

Until then, she'd have to grin, bear it and start giving the men on her *mamm*'s list a chance.

"Explain it to me again." David was looking at Nick like he had pie on his face.

Lydia merely shook her head and reached for her coffee mug, fascinated by his story. *Ya*, it was entertaining all right. The story of how he'd managed to mess up the best thing in his life. The story of how he'd become tongue-tied when asked the most important question in the universe.

"Why didn't you just correct her, Nick? It's plain you do care for her."

"*Ya*, I do, and I was going to correct her, but then before I could find the words, she walked off."

David sat back with a huff and crossed his arms. "Didn't you listen when we talked before? I told you to make your intentions plain."

"You told me to plant or get out of the field. What does that even mean?"

Lydia rolled her eyes, but she did nudge the dish of peach pie toward him. Normally he could eat several pieces of Lydia's desserts, but tonight he was pretty sure that it wouldn't settle well. Nothing was settling well. His stomach had been in turmoil for days. After seeing Deborah pass him on the road in Widower Schrock's buggy, he'd headed to his *bruder*'s. He couldn't face another moment on his farm alone.

He pushed away the pie, stood and paced the length of the kitchen several times. Finally, he sat back down, determined to be completely honest with his family.

"I thought I could wait. After my experience in Maine, with Olivia, I wasn't eager to jump back into the dating scene."

When they both nodded in understanding, he pushed on.

"I made a plan—a five-year plan for turning my land into a profitable farm and my house into a home." He stopped there, unsure how to proceed.

Gently, Lydia asked, "How is that working out for you?"

He laughed, covered his face with his hands and finally sighed. "Just fine until I met two little redheaded boys and their beautiful *mamm*. I didn't expect to fall in love."

"But you do love her?" Lydia pressed.

"For sure and certain, I do. Mind you, I wasn't looking for a relationship, and I definitely had never considered an instant family, but now they are all I can think about. And my plan... Well, it seems rather pointless if I'm the only person in it."

David and Lydia shared a look, and then they both smiled.

"Sounds to me as if you've grown up, *bruder*."

"It also sounds as if your heart has healed."

"But what do I do now? How do I...straighten this out?"

They spent the next half hour talking about courting, how to be honest with someone about your feelings, how to begin a genuine relationship and enjoy time with one another. They spoke about the importance of establishing a firm foundation, one built on honesty and hope and the future—not the past.

By the time he left their home, he was feeling better about his prospects. On the one hand, he had seen Deborah going down the road in Widower Schrock's buggy, which meant that she was allowing her *mamm* to set up dates for her. On the other hand, he already had Jacob and Joseph on his side, and he lived close to her. It would be easy to stop by with a bouquet of wildflowers or vegetables from his garden. Plus, they had a history together. He knew what she liked and what she didn't.

All he needed was for her to give him a chance.

The next day was a Saturday. He waited until he was sure that everyone would be up and about, then checked his hair in the mirror, combed it down with his fingers and called out to Blue. He'd spied purple asters growing next to the fence. He cut a few sprigs of prairie grass as well, tied them together with a ribbon that Lydia had given him and headed next door.

Deborah was in the back garden, harvesting the last of the tomatoes and green beans and peppers.

"Where are your helpers?"

She glanced up in surprise, looked at the flowers in his hand and then resumed harvesting. "Jacob and Joseph have gone to their cousin's for the day. You know Mary and Simon moved to Middlebury, and my boys have decided it's the very best place to spend their Saturday."

Nick set the flowers on the bench at the end of the garden and joined her in plucking vegetables from the plants. "How has your week been?"

Deborah reached out and scratched Blue between the ears. "My week? Okay, I suppose."

Hmm. She wasn't making this easy, and she was still tossing him quizzical looks, as if wondering what he was up to.

"Did your knitting class folks like the new pattern you shared with them?" When she raised her eyebrows in surprise, he defended himself with, "What? I listen. I even know you were going to use variegated thread."

"Yarn."

"Whatever."

The laughter seemed to set them both back on solid ground. As they finished gathering vegetables from the garden, Deborah told him about her class of knitters, which included one woman who was a beginner and couldn't quite learn how to cast on. Nick hadn't the faintest idea what that meant. It sounded like something you'd do with a rope and a boat, but then again, he'd always taken for granted that hats and scarves and sweaters simply appeared in his dresser drawers. He'd never before appreciated how much thought and work went into them.

"The shop and the class are lucky to have you there, Deborah."

"Danki." She met his gaze, smiled slightly, then stood and brushed the dirt from her apron.

He picked up the bounty of their labor, walked closer to her until there was only the basket of vegetables between them, both of their hands holding it for a moment before he passed it to her.

"I suppose I should get these things inside."

Blue lay in the dirt, staring from Deborah to Nick and giving him a look that said *what are you waiting for?*

"Could we talk for a minute?"

Deborah pulled in her bottom lip, something he'd noticed she did when unsure about a thing, but she eventually decided in his favor and nodded.

They walked to the bench, both sat and he offered her the flowers. "I thought you might enjoy these."

"I appreciate that, Nick. I really do…"

"But?"

"But…why are you doing this? We're not dating anymore."

"We're not fake dating." He reached out, tucked a stray lock of hair into her *kapp*, let his fingers linger on her cheek. When she didn't pull away, he leaned forward and kissed her softly. But he knew, from his talk with Lydia and David, that kissing wouldn't solve this. He needed to use words to tell her how he felt.

"I'm in love with you, Deborah."

Her eyes widened in astonishment. "What?"

Why was she surprised? Had he been that negligent

in letting her know how he felt? He'd thought it was so obvious.

"I don't know when it happened. It might have been when we ate pizza together on our first date—"

"Fake date."

"Or it might have been when we were kayaking."

"You nearly tipped our kayak over into the St. Joseph River."

"I can't tell you when it happened, but I can tell you that I care about you."

She looked as if she wanted to believe him. Glancing down, she ran her fingers up and down the piece of ribbon. Finally, she looked up, met his gaze. "But the other day…when I asked you…"

"I was trying to find the right words, and I'll be honest. You deserve nothing short of complete honesty from me. I was afraid. I didn't know if you felt the same."

He waited, a lump forming in his throat as she hesitated, started to speak, then stared out across the garden. When she looked up at him, his heart felt like it sank to his shoes. Was she going to turn him down? Had he imagined that she felt as he did when, in fact, she didn't?

"I care about you, too, Nick."

He wanted to jump up, grab her in his arms and twirl her around.

"But…"

There was that word again.

"I've done some serious thinking about myself, my life, even my fears of moving forward. I've spoken about all of this with my parents. I've agreed to date again…to date properly."

Widower Schrock!

"My boys deserve to have a mother who isn't afraid.

I want to be courageous and bold. I also want to be careful, for their sake as well as my own."

"You and Widower Schrock…"

She shrugged. "I barely know Nathaniel." She stared up at him. "I barely know you."

"I want to remedy that." He reached for her hand. "Would you allow me to court you…properly?"

His mouth grew dry, and the muscles in his left arm began to twitch. Was she going to say no? Had he waited too long? Was he about to pay the price for his own cowardice?

Then she looked up, smiled and said three words that caused his heart to sing. "I'd like that."

Nick knew he could do this. Deborah was worth doing it and doing it correctly. How long it took wasn't important. So what if courting Deborah pushed his five-year plan to six or seven? None of that mattered when considering a life without Deborah and Jacob and Joseph. And in that moment, he understood that Deborah wouldn't only be looking for a man who would be good to her and love and cherish her. She was also looking for a man who would be a father to her children.

Nick was determined to prove to her that he was the man for both jobs.

Chapter Eleven

Nick took Deborah to dinner that evening. They drove by her yarn shop and stopped to see the window displays she'd created. There were hats of various sizes pinned to what looked like a clothesline. Below them were sweaters that matched the hats—some on teddy bears, some on hangers, some tossed over a rocking chair. Everything was done with fall colors.

"Makes me want to buy some thread and take up knitting myself. Plus, I heard this shop has a *gut* teacher."

Deborah laughed, slipped her arm through his and explained the difference between thread and yarn. Nick noticed how her eyes lit up when she talked about her customers.

They ate at the pizza place, laughed about their first time there, then took a leisurely drive home. It was the best date of his life, and they really hadn't done anything. But they had spent time together. It was all he wanted—time with Deborah.

Sunday was a church day, and although he noticed Nathaniel Schrock talking to Deborah before the service, she didn't sit with him at lunch. She sat with Nick and his *bruder* and their *kinner*. Deborah knew David and Lydia, but they hadn't spent much time together. The women were soon talking about children, fall activities and even the upcoming Christmas season. When they'd finished the meal, Nick asked Deborah if she'd like to take a walk down by the creek. When she said yes, David gave Nick a covert thumbs-up sign.

Their courtship seemed to fall into a very natural rhythm. He looked forward to seeing her, thought about little else, and he spent time listening. Lydia had emphasized how important that was. *Don't try to solve her problems for her, Nick. Just listen.*

When Deborah described the latest antics of Jacob and Joseph, he'd only sympathized. She'd seemed surprised when he didn't tell her what she was doing wrong. She'd even called him on it. "You once told me that raising twins couldn't possibly be harder than growing up with seven younger siblings."

"I might have been seeing that from the viewpoint of a *bruder*, not a parent."

"Meaning?"

"Meaning things like raising children aren't as easy as it looks from the outside."

She'd laughed and reached for his hand. It was progress. She hadn't decided she could trust him completely, but she was giving him a chance. That was all he could or would ask for.

On school days, he made sure he was busy in the afternoons. He didn't stand by the mailbox waiting for Jacob and Joseph. He wanted to, but he also understood that he hadn't earned that spot in their lives yet.

On Tuesday, he stopped over to see her *dat* before dinner—to update him on the goats, the pigs and how they might expand their collection of animals in the spring. Bethany invited him to stay for dinner.

"I'd love to, if it's okay with Deborah." He didn't want to crowd in on her family. She needed space and time to decide what she wanted in her life and whether or not that included him.

Deborah laughed and said, "It's chicken stew—you're in for a treat."

He played ball with Jacob and Joseph as they waited for dinner, and he knew—with all his heart, he was certain—that this was what he wanted. He wanted a family. He was ready to be a *dat* and a husband.

On Wednesday there was a fairly intense storm that blew through rather quickly. Lots of wind, a little rain, and then the sun was out again. He checked the goats, worked on a portion of fence that had fallen over and brushed down Big Girl.

Late Thursday afternoon, he was adding fresh water to the pigs' mud wallow, thinking of the day the boys had helped him create it, when he looked up and saw Deborah running down his lane.

He dropped the hose, turned off the water, then met her as she stopped near the goat pen. She bent over, holding her side and pulling in deep breaths.

"What's wrong?"

"It's Jacob and Joseph…"

With those four words, it seemed as if time stopped. He didn't breathe, couldn't move, couldn't think. *It's Jacob and Joseph…*

"They didn't come home from school. I can't find them. I…I traced their route back to the schoolhouse, but everyone was gone already."

"Okay. Is there anywhere they stop along the way?"

"*Nein.* It's all fields. There are a few houses, pretty

far off the road…but the way they come home there are no other children."

"Okay." He put a hand on both of her shoulders and waited for her to look up. "We'll find them—together. Let's go back. Walk me through it, and we'll find them. They're boys. They probably got to playing somewhere and lost track of time."

She nodded. He understood that she wanted to believe him, but fear was nipping at her heels. The sun was going down, and it would be easier to find them if they could do so before dark. He glanced at the horizon, judged that they had an hour at the most, and then he pulled her into his arms.

Deborah's body trembled, and he held her tighter. "We will find them, Deborah. It's going to be all right."

He called to Blue, who joined them as they started down the lane and turned in the direction of the schoolhouse. They walked slowly, looking for any sign of two seven-year-old boys.

"Did you tell your parents?"

"Nein." She stepped around a puddle. *"Dat*'s been feeling poorly. I didn't want to worry them, and then when I couldn't find Jacob or Joseph, when I'd gone all the way to the school and back…all I could think of was coming to you."

"I'm glad you did." He hoped his smile held more confidence than he felt. Where could they have gone? Fields stretched in every direction. Farmhouses were set a good distance back from the road. There was no sign of other children. No animals that could have tempted them away from the route home.

Blue trotted along beside them. The dog didn't show any indication that he understood they were looking for the boys. Blue was an Australian cattle dog. He was bred to be energetic and work hard, and he was by nature loyal. He wasn't necessarily a tracker, though, and that was what they could use right now.

If they didn't find the boys by dark, he'd take Deborah back, tell her parents and phone the bishop. They'd call the police. Children had wandered off before. It didn't happen often, but it did happen. Their entire community would insist on being part of the search party. They would find Jacob and Joseph. He had to believe they would. His heart cried out to *Gotte*, praying that they were okay, that they weren't frightened or hurt.

And then he saw it…to the east and set back a good quarter mile. "There," he said.

Deborah stopped, frozen in place.

They stared at the dilapidated barn—old, half-fallen and close enough to the road that the boys might have seen something. Jacob might have chased something into it. A dog, maybe? If they'd glimpsed an injured animal, Joseph would have insisted on seeing if they could help it. They only had a few minutes until dark, but this felt right—it felt like the place they should search.

Deborah had been walking up and down the fence line. Blue put his nose to the ground and walked slowly in the other direction. Suddenly he began to bark, and when they looked toward him, the dog spun in a circle—then barked. Again. Deborah and Nick both ran and knelt by a T-post that held up the barbed wire. The wire had obviously been pulled apart, and sitting next to the T-post were two lunch boxes.

"Are they theirs?"

"Yes."

He held the wire apart as she ducked through, then she did the same for him. Blue had already pushed under the bottom two wires and was trotting toward the barn. Even as Nick tried not to picture what might have happened, they were running toward the structure, calling out the boys' names.

The side of the barn that was still standing was the side that offered no doors, no windows. He led the way around to the other side, to what should have been the front, but it was merely a heap of old boards and shattered windows. They continued following Blue and picking their way over the scattered debris.

"The wind did this?" Deborah's voice was a strangled whisper.

"It's been ready to go for some time. The wind simply did in ten minutes what might have taken another six months."

"If the wind caused this to happen yesterday, then it couldn't have fallen on the boys today."

"I don't know. Let's keep looking."

"They can't be here, Nick. Surely they wouldn't have…"

And then Blue barked—once and with authority. Both Nick and Deborah froze and strained to listen. A tiny meow pierced the gathering dusk.

"This way." Together they rounded the corner. If anything, this side was even worse. Nick looked down, looked at the mud and saw Joseph's footprint. Or was it Jacob's? Blue was scrambling on top of the wreckage, whining and pawing at the debris.

"Jacob. Joseph. If you can hear us, call out."

"Jacob! Joseph!" Deborah had also seen the footprint. She began pulling at boards, tearing them away, completely unaware of the abuse to her hands, frantically calling out to her children.

Nick put a hand on her arm. "Listen."

It was a cough—small, under the rubble, but un

mistakable. Blue barked twice and bounded over to Nick, then took off around the corner.

"We're coming." Deborah darted around to the other side of the rubble and resumed clawing at the boards.

"Jacob, Joseph." Nick cleared his throat, his voice gravelly with unshed tears. "Can you holler out? Let us know where you are, but don't try to move."

"Over here." The voice was followed by more coughing.

Nick was certain it was beyond the initial pile of rubble. Blue had disappeared in that direction.

"Give me your hand," he whispered to Deborah. "Try to step where I step. We go slow and carefully."

She seemed to understand the risk they were taking. Should they unsettle the pile, cause it to shift, it could hurt the boys even more. But Nick didn't think it would. He thought they were past that. He hoped, he prayed fervently, that he was right.

They climbed over the top and looked down to where Blue was lying on his belly, whimpering joyfully and licking Jacob's face.

"Jacob!" The scream that tore from Deborah nearly broke Nick's heart.

"Mamm?"

They scrambled down the pile of debris. Jacob was pinned beneath a piece of roofing. His face was covered with dirt. Tears had left paths down his cheeks. He also had blood running down his face from a cut on his forehead, but otherwise he seemed unhurt.

Nick lifted up a corner of the roofing and saw that there was maybe a three-inch clearing between it and a fallen roof brace. "Do your legs hurt, Jacob?"

"Nein." He wiggled his feet. "I'm just… I'm stuck."

"Okay. On three, I'm going to lift, and your *mamm* is

going to tug on your legs and pull you free. If anything feels like it's broken, if you feel any sudden pain, you holler out, Jacob, and we'll stop. We'll think of something else. Got it?"

"*Ya.*"

Blue took three steps back and sat. Nick pulled in a very deep breath and planted his feet. "One, two, three…" Sweat bathed his forehead as he fought to lift and hold the section of roofing.

"He's free," Deborah called. "Jacob, oh, Jacob."

Blue bathed the boy with kisses, and Jacob slung one arm around the dog's neck and the other around his mother's.

"Where's Joseph?" she asked.

"That way." Jacob inclined his head to the south side of the structure. "He was talking to me, but then…" Tears caught in his throat, but he pushed on. "Then he stopped."

"I'll look," Nick said. "Stay with Jacob."

Deborah remained kneeling beside Jacob, touching him, kissing his face, telling him everything was going to be all right now that they'd found him. "We'll get Joseph out. We'll be home before you know it."

He glanced back in time to see her pull the boy into her arms. Nick closed his eyes, and tears cascaded down his cheeks. His heart was filled with joy that they'd found Jacob and fear that Joseph was badly hurt— possibly even unconscious.

He turned his attention to the direction that Jacob had indicated. Blue, apparently understanding that his work wasn't done, joined the search for Joseph. Nick was reminded of the childhood game of pick-up sticks, only this time there was more to lose than a game. This time Joseph's life might depend on their actions

He walked slowly around the large pile and spotted the boy at the same moment that Blue did. Joseph lay near the edge of the debris, under a portion of wall that had collapsed. Next to him was a small kitten, tucked under the boy's arm, looking frightened and thin. Nick scrambled around the debris until he was kneeling beside him. Blue commenced licking Joseph's face and whined softly whenever the kitten glanced in his direction. Joseph wasn't aware of any of it. His eyes were closed, and he lay perfectly still. Nick reached over, laid his fingers against the artery in the boy's neck and felt a pulse. Hope rose in his heart like a bird taking flight.

"I've got him, Deborah. Stay where you are. I'm going to try to…" But she was already at his side, exclaiming over her son, who still didn't stir.

"He's going to be okay."

"I know. I know he will be." She swiped at her tears. "Should I run for help?"

How long would it take? Thirty minutes? An hour? Did Joseph have that long? Nick had no idea what was wrong with the boy. He stared at the wall that had pinned him to the ground. There was only the one piece. It wasn't a pile like Jacob had been pinned under.

"Let's try first. If we can't do it, then I'll run for help while you stay with them."

She nodded in agreement.

"I'm going out the way we came and in through…" He pointed to where the last ray of sunlight was piercing the other side of the rubble. "I'll lift from there, and you lift from here."

"And I'll pull out Joseph."

Nick hadn't heard Jacob walk up. He looked small,

exhausted and scared, but his expression was one of pure determination. "I want to help."

"Okay. Wait for my signal."

To Deborah, it seemed as if freeing her son took a lifetime, and it also happened more quickly than a heartbeat. Nick was standing on the opposite side, again planting his feet and squatting to grab the portion of fallen wall.

"With me... One, two, three."

She tried to lift when he said *three*, tried with all her might to pull up on the section pinning her son. It looked as if it didn't move at all, and then there was a slight change. Deborah dug in, prayed for the strength of a thousand warriors and pulled up on the section of wall.

Her voice came out a ragged whisper. It seemed to rise up from deep in her soul. "Now, Jacob."

She looked across at Nick. His face had turned a dark red, and she knew they had a few seconds, no more.

"He's free. I got him."

She dropped the section at the same time that Nick did. Dust rose up from the pile, and Blue jumped back. The kitten scooted farther into Joseph's jacket. Joseph didn't so much as blink.

"Is he okay?" Jacob asked.

Deborah was afraid to move him, afraid something was broken. She touched his face, ran her hands down his arms, checked his legs. Everything seemed okay, so why didn't he open his eyes? What was wrong?

"He's unconscious." Nick's voice was soft in her ear. "I don't think we'll make matters worse by lifting him."

"Okay." She turned to Jacob and noticed the gash on his forehead. Had she seen it before? How could she have missed it?

She reached for the hem of her apron, tried to rip off a piece, but she couldn't make the fabric tear. Nick pulled a pocketknife out of his pocket and poked a hole in the fabric. She tore it free, then wrapped it around Jacob's head, at least temporarily stanching the flow of blood.

"Okay," she said. "Let's get out of here."

Jacob picked up the kitten.

Deborah reached out for Jacob, who slid his small hand into hers. Nick picked up Joseph, who still hadn't stirred. Blue stood just outside the shadow of the structure. The last of the day's light had fled, and darkness was coming.

They would get Joseph home.

He would wake up. He had to wake up.

They crossed the field to the portion of fence where they'd climbed through only a few minutes earlier. Jacob ducked in between the wires and knelt by their lunch boxes, settling the kitten inside his before snapping the lid shut. "Just for a few minutes," he whispered.

"Hold the wire for your *mamm*, Jacob."

He did, Deborah crept through and then Nick handed Joseph over to her. In that moment when both of their hands were supporting the weight of her son, Nick's eyes met hers, and she knew, she truly believed, that some good would come of this. She silently promised herself, promised *Gotte* and her boys, that she would never again take another moment with them for granted.

Nick ducked through the fence, took Joseph back into his arms and gave her a weak smile. Blue was already on the road, waiting for them, leading the way home.

They hurried into a darkness that had now completely cloaked the fields. They practically sprinted down the road, back to the lane and to her parents' house. She was barely aware of collapsing on the porch, of her *mamm* and *dat* running out to see what was wrong, of Nick harnessing Rhapsody to the buggy. One minute she was standing in front of their porch, so very grateful to be home. The next moment Rhapsody was headed down the road at a quick trot—all six of them, plus one dog and one kitten, crammed into the buggy.

The next several hours passed in a blur, and yet Deborah understood that it was a night that would remain in her memory if she lived to be one hundred. Jacob needed four stitches in his forehead, but otherwise he was fine. Joseph's situation was more complicated. A nurse had started an IV in his arm.

"I ordered the IV because Joseph seems somewhat dehydrated," Dr. Cramer explained. She was about Deborah's height, with short black hair. Her manner was patient, understanding, even.

"When will he wake up?"

"In approximately ten percent of concussions, the person is rendered unconscious for a time. I'd like to do a CT scan to make sure there's no bleeding in his brain. We'll have those results back pretty quickly, and then we'll talk again."

Deborah nodded as if she understood what the doctor had said. CT scan? Bleeding in his brain? She reached for her *mamm*'s hand, clung to it. Her parents had both been amazingly calm throughout the entire ordeal. Concerned, but also certain that Joseph would be fine.

Once they wheeled Joseph out of the room, her *mamm* stood. "I'll take Jacob to sit with your *dat*. No doubt, he'd like a *gut*, rousing game of checkers."

"Think we could eat first?" Jacob asked. "Or…"

He turned to look at where his *bruder* had been,

then at his *mamm*. "Maybe I should wait until Joseph can eat?"

Deborah squatted in front of him. "Joseph is going to be fine, and he'd want you to go ahead and have some supper. You need to keep up your strength."

"Ya?"

"Sure and certain. Joseph may need help at first, so he'll be depending on you."

"Okay."

He flung his arms around her neck, and she felt his hot tears against her skin. A surge of love pierced Deborah's heart, reminding her of the day they were born, when the midwife had first placed both boys in her arms and she had wondered at the miracle of their birth.

Jacob pulled back and swiped the sleeve of his shirt across his eyes. The nurse had cleaned up around the cut on his forehead, but the rest of his face still held layers of dirt and sweat and tears.

"Go with your *mammi*. I'll send word as soon as we know anything else."

Deborah's *mamm* was at the door when Deborah called out to her, "Could you ask Nick to come back?"

"Of course."

She couldn't have said if two minutes had passed or twenty. Suddenly Nick was standing in front of her, and she could no longer hold back the tears that had been building since she'd first realized that her boys were missing. She lurched out of the chair and into his arms. She wept until her emotions were spent.

Nick didn't tell her to stop crying.

He didn't pretend to know what was going to happen next.

He simply held her.

Finally, she collapsed into the chair and dried her face with the torn hem of her apron. He walked over to the sink, found a washcloth in the cabinet next to it and soaked it in warm water. Wringing it out, he snagged a hand towel and brought them both back to her.

"Danki."

"Gem gschehne."

She pressed the warm cloth to her eyes, then scrubbed at her face. Handing the cloth back to Nick, she patted everything dry. Then she reached for Nick's hand. He interlaced his fingers with hers and they sat there, waiting and praying, hoping. Believing.

An hour later, an orderly rolled Joseph's bed back into the room. She heard his voice even before she saw his red hair. She heard his voice, and suddenly she could breathe again. Hopping to her feet, she tried to scoot around the bed as they pushed it into the room.

Joseph smiled at her, and Deborah didn't know if there'd ever been a more beautiful sight. "You're awake."

He waved a small hand at her.

"Oh, Joseph. You're awake. How do you feel?"

"Okay. That machine they put me in was pretty cool, *Mamm.*"

The orderly repositioned his IV bag on the pole and told them the doctor would be in soon.

Deborah looked at Nick and understood that he was waiting, not wanting to intrude. She nodded at him— just a short, brief gesture, but it was all he needed. He popped out of his chair and stood on the other side of the hospital bed.

"Hey, Nick."

"Hey, Joseph."

"Is Blue here? I had a dream about him. He was licking my face."

"He is here, but we had to leave him in the buggy."

"And the kitten?"

"Also in the buggy, but lying on the blanket under the seat."

"So the kitten is safe?"

"Very. Blue learned his lesson with cats long ago. He won't bother your kitten."

All this talk about a stray cat! Her son had been returned to her. Her son was going to be okay. Deborah straightened his cover, patted his hand and again kissed his forehead. "How do you feel? Does your head hurt?"

"*Ya*, and the lights seem awfully bright in here."

"We can fix that." Dr. Cramer stood in the door to the room. She reached over and switched off the light directly over Joseph's bed. "How's that?"

"Better."

The doctor remained in the doorway, staring down at her tablet. Finally, she looked up, smiled and said, "Good to meet you, Joseph."

Joseph looked at Deborah.

"This is your doctor—Dr. Cramer. She's helping you get well."

Dr. Cramer walked next to the bed, pulled up a chair and sat. "Can you tell me what happened, Joseph?"

"I woke up, right as they were putting me in the brain machine."

"And before that?"

He shook his head, stared at the ceiling a minute, then closed his eyes. "Jacob and I were walking home, and I saw a little kitten—sitting by the side of the road and crying. We tried to catch it, to bring it home..." He stopped, looked at Deborah. "We were going to ask first, of course, but we couldn't just leave it there and go back. We might never find it again."

She nodded once, and he resumed his story.

"The kitten ran into an old barn, under some boards. Jacob was on one side, and I was on the other. We thought we could tease her out, but then…then there was a rumble, like thunder, and…and I don't remember anything else until I woke up a few minutes ago."

"The barn fell down, Joseph." Deborah shook her head in wonder.

Nick was now standing behind Deborah. He let out a long sigh—an expression of wonder and gratitude and disbelief all combined together. "I suspect it was leaning anyway from the storm that came through the day before. When you were searching for the cat, you must have bumped into the one thing that was keeping it propped up."

Joseph shrugged. "Maybe I'm glad I don't remember that part."

"Cat, huh?" The doctor smiled and set down her tablet. "Next time maybe fetch a can of tuna and wait for the cat to come to you."

Dr. Cramer spent the next fifteen minutes checking Joseph's vision, balance and cognitive functions. She pronounced him a healthy seven-year-old with a big bump on his head and most certainly a concussion. "He's passed all of my tests, the CT scan looks good and he's keeping down the juice we gave him. Let's give it two more hours, make sure he can eat, and then we'll send him home."

Everyone smiled at that. The doctor said she'd be back in a couple hours and to call the nurse if they needed anything.

Nick had sunk into the chair the doctor had vacated.

Deborah tapped him on the shoulder. "Would you mind staying here a few minutes?"

"Nowhere I'd rather be." And something in his voice convinced Deborah that he meant it.

That and the tender look he gave her sent shivers down her arms. She wanted to explore that, to consider what Nick's words and his actions of this evening meant. But she was too tired. She would be lucky to make it through the next few hours without falling asleep.

"I'll be quick. I want to tell *Mamm* and *Dat* the *gut* news."

"And Jacob. Don't forget to tell him." Joseph yawned. "I think he worries about me."

"I'll be sure to tell Jacob, too."

When she reached the door to the room, she glanced back. Nick was sitting by the hospital bed, right foot propped over his left knee. She could tell by the words she caught here and there that he was describing Blue's help in the search and rescue.

Deborah glanced down at her hands—torn and bruised from trying to dig her sons out from beneath a pile of rubble. Her apron was tattered, and she didn't want to think about what her *kapp*, hair and face looked like. Nick glanced up and smiled. He had dirt smudged across his face, and she knew that if she looked, his hands would be as dirty and bruised as hers.

It had been a long day, an eternity if measured in fears and hopes, but something told Deborah that it was also the day she would always look back on as the beginning of the rest of her life.

Chapter Twelve

Nick realized he was not the person he used to be. That Nick—the old Nick—might have been scared off by the incident with Jacob and Joseph and the Old Leaning Barn. That was the way the boys referred to the incident, always emphasized as if they'd used capital letters and written a story about it. Actually, Joseph did write a story about it once they returned to school, and Jacob once again drew the picture.

In the drawing, Blue and the kitten peeked out from a leaning stick barn. Deborah stood next to the barn, her stick arms reaching out to gather the boys to her. And beside the barn was Nick, larger than the barn itself, a smile on his face as his stick arms reached out to lift the barn.

This time, Deborah didn't become upset that he was included in the picture. She handed it to him and said, "Put it on your refrigerator. I'm not likely to forget that day."

Both Jacob and Joseph seemed to have recovered quite quickly from the incident.

Deborah was another matter. She was quieter, a bit more pensive, and Nick wasn't exactly sure what she was thinking. He tried to give her space while at the same time assuring her that he was there for her. It was a fine line to walk, but she was worth the effort.

The last weekend in September, he offered to take the boys to town to see the Six Horse Hitch Classic Series World Finals.

"You wouldn't mind?"

"Of course not. I'd enjoy it, and I think they would, too." He hesitated, and then asked, "Would you like to go with us?"

"I would, but..."

He didn't even attempt to finish that sentence for her, didn't push, simply waited.

"*Dat* doesn't seem quite himself," she admitted. "I think I'd like to stay here and help around the house, maybe give *Mamm* a few hours to run errands or visit a friend."

They were sitting on the steps of the front porch. Nick was thinking about the time he'd stormed over and offered to show her how to raise twins. What an arrogant thing to suggest.

"I'm sorry," he said.

"For what?"

"For thinking I knew how to do things better than you." He shook his head at what a fool he'd been. "You're doing a *gut* job, you know."

"I am? With what?" She raised her eyebrows and dared him to go on.

"With your life, your parents and most especially the boys."

Deborah laughed and leaned her head against his shoulder.

They sat that way awhile, just enjoying a beautiful Saturday morning and the company of one another. The quiet scene was broken when Oliver, the new kitten, tore around the corner of the house, paused and hissed at Blue, then scampered under the porch. Blue plopped into the dirt at their feet, head on his paws, one eye on the kitten, the other drifting shut so that it looked as if he was winking at the feline.

The boys arrived seconds later, trying to tempt the kitten out with a piece of yarn. Blue attacked the yarn, and the cat scampered out and ran up Jacob's pant leg, causing him to yelp and laugh at the same time. Joseph lavished attention on Blue, throwing his arms around the dog and knocking over a flowerpot in the process.

Deborah sat up and said with a laugh, "They're all yours. Bring them back before Christmas."

The afternoon was quite nearly perfect. As Nick and the boys drove into Shipshe, he noticed the brightness of the day, the falling leaves, even the pumpkin displays in the Amish and *Englisch* yards they passed. Parking took a few minutes, but they were able to find a seat where they could see the finish line. The boys were amazed at the size and power of the horses.

Joseph stared at them in fascination. "Why are they so much bigger than Rhapsody, Nick?"

"They're work horses, what we call draft horses. Surely you've seen them during the harvest."

"I guess we have," Jacob said.

"Maybe last year, but we were just kids then."

Jacob tossed his ball in the air, the baseball that was always in his pocket, then smiled. "Kids don't notice things like the size of horses."

They cheered mightily for all the teams and laughed when the older Amish gentleman who won stood and took a bow. The crowd dispersed, but it seemed no one was in a hurry to go home. Nick thought that perhaps

Deborah could use another hour alone, so he bought them cotton candy. They walked through the crowd, greeting church members and smiling knowingly at one another when *Englisch* tourists attempted to snap a covert picture. Nick realized that Shipshe was a *gut* place to grow up—always had been. Yes, the larger world occasionally crowded in, but that wasn't always a bad thing. The boys would learn how to live a plain and simple life in the middle of the twenty-first century. He hoped he would be there to help them with that.

As they were headed toward home, the boys put their heads together and whispered for a moment. Apparently, Joseph was deemed the one to ask the question. He sat up straighter, cleared his throat and said, "We'd like to know your intentions toward our *mamm*."

Nick almost choked on the soda he'd taken a drink from. "My intentions?"

"We'll be honest with you, Nick." Jacob tossed the ball from his right hand to his left—back and forth, back and forth. "My *bruder* and I don't actually know what the word *intentions* means, but we've heard it plenty."

"We happened to be, uh, listening in the last time Nathaniel Schrock came to pick up *Mamm*. He told her that his intentions were honorable." Joseph pulled off his straw hat, scratched his head, causing his red hair to stand on end, then replaced the hat. "What does that mean exactly?"

Wow.

Nick couldn't think of a more uncomfortable conversation to have with two seven-year-old boys, other than the birds and the bees. Though if his relationship with Deborah progressed as he hoped it would, that might be his job one day. Not today, though. Not when they were only seven. Suddenly he was grateful that this conversation wasn't that one.

"Okay. Well. Intentions refer to our goals or purpose."

The boys looked at each other and then shook their heads.

Nick tried to think of a way to bring the topic down to their level. "Jacob, why do you toss that ball constantly?"

"Missed one in the outfield last week. I want to get better."

"Okay, so your intention is to improve your ball-playing skills."

"Sure."

Joseph sat up straighter. "And when I practice my letters on an assignment, my intention is to write better."

"Exactly." Nick felt rather proud of himself. He'd handled that well.

He reached for his soda cup, took another sip through the straw and spewed it when Joseph asked, "So what is your intention? What are you trying to get better at? And what is Nathaniel's intention?"

Was Deborah still seeing Nathaniel Schrock? They hadn't talked about courting exclusively, but he'd assumed…

Nick felt sweat break out on his forehead. This was like being grilled by a boss when applying for a job. "I suppose I'm trying to learn how to be a better friend to your *mamm*. I can't speak for Nathaniel. You'd have to check with him."

"Fair enough. I guess you have to ask a person a thing if you want to know. Otherwise, you can't really be sure of what another person is thinking…" Jacob bumped his shoulder into Joseph's. "Unless you're a twin."

Which started both boys laughing, and like a sudden shift in the wind, their attention turned to Blue and Oliver the kitten and schoolmates.

Leaving Nick with their question circling in his mind. He knew his intention, had known it since Deborah had broken off their fake dating. He'd been trying to give her time and space. Although that had only been a few weeks ago, it seemed much longer. So many things had happened. So much had changed between them. They'd grown closer, given what they'd been through together.

Perhaps he'd waited long enough.

Maybe it was time to broach the subject with Deborah. Maybe it was time to make his intentions known.

The next day was an off-Sunday, meaning the community didn't meet for a church service. Instead, families and neighbors gathered for a meal and to catch up on recent events. Deborah was relieved to have a day off to spend at home. She felt as if she could lie down and take a nap for hours upon hours. Of course, she didn't.

They'd prepared for the meal the day before. The boys were quite excited about showing Oliver off to their cousin Christopher. Her parents had invited Nick to join them as well. It made for a nice, medium-sized group—six adults and three children. They ate lunch on the front porch, since it was a stormy day. The soft patter of rain on the roof soothed Deborah's soul and calmed her spirit. The boys were playing in the barn— their solid, safe barn. They'd taken off with Blue and Oliver, promising to be careful.

Deborah's brother Simon and Nick were discussing

the upcoming harvest, plans for the next spring and the merits of buying versus borrowing draft horses. Her *dat* listened and nodded occasionally.

"Where did your *mamm* go?" Mary asked. They were standing at the kitchen sink, washing and rinsing the lunch dishes.

"Said she wanted to lie down for a few minutes."

"Is she okay?"

"I guess." Deborah's hands stilled in the water. She leaned forward to peer out the kitchen window, to better see the men where they sat on the porch. Watching her *dat*, she sensed that something had changed, but she couldn't put her finger on exactly what was different. He looked the same, though he wasn't as involved as he usually was. It was almost as if he was only partly with them.

Mary crowded in to see what she was staring at. "And your *dat*?"

"I don't know," Deborah answered honestly. "He hasn't been himself these last few days."

"Should he go to the doctor?"

"*Mamm* suggested it last night. He said that if he ran to the doctor every time he felt tired, he'd never get a thing done."

"Oh, dear."

"She'll wear him down. *Mamm* usually wins in health matters. She's like a slow, solid drip of water on a rock, leaving its impression until the rock has no idea what happened to it."

Mary laughed. "We all need someone like that in our lives. I suppose in my home it was my oldest *schweschder*. She'd pop us into the buggy at the first sign of fever."

They finished cleaning the dishes, then wiped down

the counters. They spoke of their boys, school days, the coming harvest, even Christmas plans. Since many of their gifts were homemade, it was something best started on in October. Deborah realized with a shock that October was right around the corner. Where had the month gone?

She and Mary walked to the barn, carrying a tin full of cookies, a thermos of milk and a stack of five plastic cups. The boys paused in their game of tag long enough to swig down the milk and stuff extra cookies into their pockets, then they were off again.

Mary nodded toward the hayloft and raised her eyebrows. Deborah laughed. "Sure. Why not?"

It was while they were sitting there, their feet hanging over the edge and swinging back and forth, that Mary asked about her courting.

"Still seeing Nathaniel?"

"Nein." Deborah smiled. "He's a nice person, but there's no spark between us."

"Spark, huh?"

"You know what I mean."

"I do indeed." They could just see out the barn doors to the porch, where the men were sitting. "I still feel that spark with your *bruder.*"

"You don't say? Even after all these years?"

"Even so." Mary flopped onto her back.

Deborah did the same, staring up at cobwebs in the corners of the ceiling. "Nick told me he loves me."

"What?" Mary popped up and stared at her in surprise. "When did this happen? When were you going to tell me? What did you say?"

"I said that I cared about him, too."

"Ouch. That's it?"

"Some days I'm not sure I believe in love anymore—

romantic love, I mean. Then I watch you and Simon, and I realize that a part of my heart still does."

"And do you love Nick?"

"Maybe. I think I could, but it's…well, it's scary to admit."

"It can be."

"After the talk with my parents—remember, I told you about that…"

Mary nodded.

"I promised myself I would live courageously. That I wouldn't hide any longer inside my parents' house. That I'd put my heart out there, if for no other reason than so my boys might have a normal home."

"Oh, Deborah."

Deborah looked over in surprise at Mary. "You sound so melancholy. What did I say?"

Mary sat up, staring down at the floor now. It seemed that she was determined to choose her words very carefully. Deborah sat up, too—interested, needing to know what her sister-in-law thought. They were the closest of friends. Deborah really did look up to her, and she admired the relationship that Mary had with Simon. She wanted that sort of relationship, that kind of home.

Clearing her throat, Mary said, "It's only that I don't think you can decide to fall in love for the sake of your boys. We can do a lot of things for our children, but I'm not sure that's one."

"Then what do I do?"

"Listen to your heart…and whatever you decide, decide it based on your needs and feelings. It's okay to do what is right and true for you. Of course, you always consider your children in your decisions, but your feelings for Nick? Well, that's something between the two of you. For a moment, I think, you have to stop being a *mamm* and simply be a woman."

"What if I don't know how to do that?"

Mary reached for her hand and plopped back down on her back. "It's rather like riding a bike. You might be wobbly at first, but eventually it will come back to you."

Did she believe that? Could she become the young girl she had been before Gavin had rejected her? She had no desire to be that young, naive girl again, but maybe she could take that girl's dreams—her dreams—and embrace them in a new way.

The rest of the afternoon passed pleasantly.

The rain stopped, the sun came out and everyone except her parents went for a walk to the back pond. Deborah watched Simon and Mary together. She watched Nick with her boys, and she wondered if she had the courage to simply be a woman, even for a little while.

The timing seemed all wrong.

Her *dat* needed to see the doctor. Her *mamm* was looking exhausted. The boys, as always, were a handful.

But perhaps love didn't wait for the perfect moment.

Maybe, just maybe, the perfect moment was the one when you decided to step out in faith.

Chapter Thirteen

Nick walked through a field, parting the tall stalks of corn as he searched. He could hear Jacob and Joseph laughing, but he couldn't see them. Occasionally a stalk would move, followed by the sound of small feet running. He wanted to call out to them, to tell them to be careful. He wanted to find them to assure himself they were all right. He parted two of the stalks, but instead of the boys, he found Deborah. She was sitting cross-legged, her head down, hands covering her face, crying.

"The boys are okay."

She shook her head and continued to weep.

He knelt in front of her. "I just heard them. They're only playing a game. They're fine."

Now she looked up, and his heart began to pound in his chest as if he'd been the one running. Something was wrong. Something was very wrong, and he needed to help her.

But then he was in the barn, alone, brushing Big Girl.

The mare was restless, more nervous than he'd ever seen her.

"Whoa, girl. Easy."

The mare looked at him, terror in her eyes, then tossed her head back, straining against the lead rope.

Nick needed to do something, but what?

He heard a high-pitched sound. His heart rate accelerated again, sweat dripped down his back and he felt real fear. There was something he needed to do. Somewhere he needed to be. Big Girl neighed loudly and then nudged him, putting her muzzle in his hand, licking his hand.

And that was what woke him. Only it wasn't Big Girl. It was Blue—sitting beside the bed and licking Nick's hand, whining and waiting.

He sat up, trying to push away the dream, the fear, and that was when he realized the ringing in his ears was actually the sound of an *Englisch* ambulance. He lurched to his feet, and Blue ran from the bed down the hall and to the front door, barking loudly.

"*Ya.* I understand." He pulled on a pair of pants, yanked the suspenders over the nightshirt he slept in, stuffed his feet into his shoes and ran out the door.

The ambulance had stopped at the Mast place. Its siren continued to blare, and Nick could see the red emergency lights piercing the darkness.

Blue kept pace with him as he dashed to the fence and through the gate. He silently thanked the Lord that they had put the pass-through there. By the time he made it to the front of the Mast home, Deborah was standing on the porch. Both boys held tight to her hands. The paramedics were loading John into the back of the ambulance. Nick had one glimpse inside, just long enough to see Bethany sitting beside her husband and an oxygen mask over his face. One paramedic climbed up into the back of the vehicle and beside the gurney, and the other slapped the door shut and jumped into the driver's seat. They headed back down the lane and to the main road, turning toward town.

Nick pivoted back toward the house in time to see Deborah sink onto the top porch step.

Blue had dropped to the ground, head resting on his paws, his gaze firmly locked on the boys.

Jacob and Joseph were uncharacteristically silent.

Nick walked closer to the small family huddled on the porch. "What happened?"

"I don't know." Deborah's voice trembled, and she pulled the boys tight against her side. "I woke to *Mamm* hollering. She told me to run to the phone shack, to call 911. By the time I got back, *Dat* was clearly in distress, clutching his arm and struggling to pull in a deep breath."

"Okay." He stepped in front of her and squatted so that they would be eye to eye.

The boys were watching him now, tears streaking their faces. He thought the fear reflected there might be the saddest thing he'd ever seen. It reminded him of his dream—of looking for the boys and for Deborah, of trying to calm his mare. The boys' expression reminded him of the very real fear he'd felt, and the way his heart had beat so hard in his chest it had actually hurt.

He put out a hand for each boy, and they grabbed it as if they were drowning. He didn't even ask if they wanted to pray, he simply closed his eyes and voiced what they had to all be thinking.

"*Gotte*, please be with John at this moment. Keep his heart beating strong. Guide their path to the hospital. May Your hand be upon him, upon Bethany, and may You guide the paramedics and nurses and doctors. *Danki* that Deborah was here to run for the phone, that the boys were here to support their *mamm*. Grant us wisdom and peace and guidance in the coming days."

The boys swiped at their eyes.

Deborah whispered, *"Danki."*

And then she told Jacob and Joseph to go inside, to put on school clothes and grab their books.

"We're going to school?" Jacob's eyes widened in surprise.

Joseph put a hand on his *mamm*'s shoulder. "We want to go to the hospital."

"We will. All of us will…" She hesitated and then looked up at Nick.

He nodded. Of course he'd go with them.

Deborah stood, smoothing down her nightgown and pulling her sweater more closely around her. "You may go to school, but you'll be going late, if at all. First, you'll go to the hospital with me and Nick."

The boys nodded solemnly, paused to shower Blue with attention, then hurried off to their rooms. The screen door had barely slammed behind them when Deborah walked into Nick's arms, and that was when his heart rate finally slowed. Deborah in his arms. The boys upstairs dressing. They were the most important people in the world to him, and he would do anything to protect their family and their home.

"It's going to be okay."

"You don't know that."

"True, but I believe it."

She pulled back enough to look up into his face, then snuggled in against him. "I'm glad you're here. I'm glad I don't have to face this alone."

He wanted to say several things.

I'll always be here.

I love you, and I love your boys.

Marry me.

He didn't. Instead, he kissed the top of her head and whispered, "I'll hitch Rhapsody up and meet you back here."

"They won't let us in until they get *Dat* settled. You have time to go home and finish dressing." There was a hint of amusement in her voice even as she pulled in a shaky breath.

"Oh, yeah. A proper shirt would probably be *gut*."

"And socks."

"That, too." He cradled her face in his hands, kissed her lips softly and thumbed away the tears still leaking from her eyes. "If I'm going home, I might as well hitch up Big Girl. She enjoys a nighttime drive."

"It's nearly morning."

He glanced east and saw she was right. On the horizon the sky was lightening ever so gently, the sun's rays sending out the barest of pink and lavender streaks. He kissed her again, then hurried home, thinking that the coming sunrise would splash across the first day of the rest of his life—the rest of his life with Deborah and Jacob and Joseph, with Bethany and John.

The dream and the emergency and the look on their faces—it had all combined to banish any last question. It didn't really matter if he could provide a perfect home. He no longer cared if his five-year plan urged caution. What mattered was the love he felt in his heart.

They made it to the hospital in record time—Big Girl tossing her head the entire way.

"Your mare is fast, Nick." Jacob sat back against the seat. "*Gut* thing you were here to drive us."

Deborah turned and scowled at her boys, who were sitting in the back seats. "I can drive a mare."

"*Ya.* You can, but it takes you a lot longer to hitch one up," Jacob pointed out.

"And we're still too short." Joseph sounded as if it was a crime that they hadn't grown to their full height yet.

Deborah reached out and tousled their red hair, then turned back around in the seat. Nick could sense that everyone was feeling better, definitely less shaky, but they were all still worried.

By the time they reached the hospital, Bishop Ezekiel was already in the waiting room. Nick didn't ask how he'd managed to beat them there. When had anyone had time to call him? All moot points. The man was here, and Nick was glad he was.

"I just spoke with Bethany." He motioned toward a sitting area. A few other people were waiting in the chairs, but they walked to a far corner where they'd have a bit of privacy.

"As you can guess, it looks like your *dat* had a heart attack. The *gut* news is that you and your *mamm* acted quickly. The doctors are stabilizing him now, and his heart doctor will be out to update us as soon as possible."

It was Jacob who voiced the question they were all wondering. "Can we see him?"

"Not yet. For now, let's sit, wait and pray."

Which was exactly what they did. Within an hour, the waiting room was full with Deborah's *bruders* and *schweschdern*, nieces and nephews. They'd brought thermoses of coffee, containers of milk and several types of baked goods—homemade cookies and brownies and granola bars. Mary, Deborah's *schweschder*-in-law, herded the children off to another part of the waiting room so the adults could talk without little ears craning to hear every word. The children sat in a circle as if they were about to play Duck, Duck, Goose. But instead of games, they quietly accepted the light breakfast.

Everyone was in shock, though this wasn't completely unexpected. It was only that they'd hoped that her *dat* was growing stronger. No one had dared to express any concern about a setback.

Had there been symptoms?

Nick didn't remember John seeming more tired or weaker.

He was thinking of that, wondering if he should have paid closer attention, when a middle-aged woman wearing a doctor's lab coat walked out and headed straight toward the family. The name stitched on her coat was Dr. Green.

"Your father has suffered a myocardial infarction."

"A heart attack?" Simon rubbed a hand up and down his face. "I knew he needed to slow down. He won't listen."

"How's he doing?" Deborah crossed her arms, then uncrossed them. "And what's next?"

"I ordered some blood work. We also performed a noninvasive echocardiogram and a cardiac cath. We were able to determine the severity and location of arterial blockage. Fortunately, it doesn't require open-heart surgery. Instead, I'd like to put in a stent to open the affected arteries."

"What exactly does that involve?" Simon asked.

"Think of the artery as a straw. Sometimes the blockage becomes so advanced that it keeps the blood from flowing through. We put in a stent to prop the artery open."

Simon looked around the circle, which included Ezekiel. Each person nodded in agreement. Nick felt a surge of relief. They wouldn't need to do open-heart surgery. He knew that was a good sign.

"Okay," Simon said. "*Ya.* Let's do the stent."

"Excellent."

Deborah sighed in relief. "When can he come home?"

"As long as his condition remains stable? He should be home tomorrow."

There were shouts of *hallelujah* and *amen* at that.

"But he is going to need to take it easy," Dr. Green cautioned. "Exercise is important, but he needs to start slowly and build his strength. What he eats is also important—less red meat and salt, more fruits and vegetables. But what's most critical at this point is that he not overdo it. And I want him in my office for a checkup at regular intervals. We may need to adjust his medicine, depending on how he's responding."

They all nodded gravely.

One way or another, they would see that John followed the doctor's orders. As they resettled in the waiting room chairs, Nick felt proud that the Masts had included him as if he were part of the family. None of Deborah's siblings lived as close as Nick did. He could be there every morning and every night. He would be there. He'd be a *gut* neighbor, and hopefully—once things were settled and Deborah had recovered from this latest blow—he'd be more than a neighbor. If she would have him, if she felt as he did, Nick was ready to officially be a part of this family.

The next week passed in something of a blur for Deborah. Her *dat*'s condition was addressed with two stents. He was able to go home three days after his attack, on the following Saturday. Deborah went to church with the boys on Sunday, but her parents stayed home. She was astonished when every single person in their congregation stopped by to speak with her.

They offered meals.

They volunteered to care for the fields and the animals.

They vowed to pray for her and the boys and her parents.

Deborah had always felt at home in her church, even after she'd left for Ohio, considered becoming Mennonite and returned as a single mom. She believed that most people accepted her back into the fold, though no doubt a few privately judged her. She was okay with that. She still occasionally judged herself for her missteps, but then she'd watch Jacob catching a frog or Joseph playing with Blue and she'd thank *Gotte* for the blessings He'd brought from those very same missteps.

On the Sunday after her *dat*'s heart attack, something in Deborah shifted. She no longer felt as if she was on the outer fringe of her community. She realized she was an important member of it—every man, woman and child was. She understood, maybe for the first time, that a church was a family of people—complete with their talents, their weaknesses and, yes, their missteps.

"You're having very serious thoughts over there." Nick nudged her foot with his under the picnic table.

They were sitting at a table with other young couples—most married and a few others who had made known their intention to marry. She and Nick hadn't done that. They hadn't really talked about where their relationship was going.

Were they a couple?

She thought of the way he'd kissed her as they'd stood in front of her parents' home, the sun just peeking over the horizon and her *dat* on the way to the hospital. She remembered the comfort of his arms around her. She considered the way he'd been there for them, almost as if he was a part of the family.

Deborah glanced up and smiled. "I suppose I was."

"Care to share?"

She shook her head, then tacked on a "Maybe later."

And she did, later, when the boys were playing with the other *kinner* and she and Nick were walking along the creek. October had arrived in a flurry of color—crops to be harvested, trees losing their leaves, the sky a bright blue. Soon it would be winter, then Christmas and then another year passed. She pulled in a deep breath, and bared the burdens of her soul to this man that she was falling in love with.

She told him how her father's health scare had helped her to appreciate her community, her neighbors, her family and him.

"Ya?" He entwined his fingers with hers.

She liked that about Nick. He enjoyed holding hands, or nudging shoulders or sitting side by side. He liked being close to her, and he seemed to draw some strength from her, as she did from him.

"More serious thoughts? I can practically hear your brain churning."

She almost held back, almost pushed the questions down to wrestle with later that night. But what was the point of doing that? Life was short—her *dat*'s illness had brought that fact home quite clearly. What was she waiting for?

"I was thinking that our *freinden*, they're all either married or planning to marry."

"Hmm." Nick rubbed his chin thoughtfully. "Can't

say as I've noticed." He easily sidestepped her playful swipe. "That means you're saying…"

"I'm not saying anything," Deborah protested. "I've never been quite in step with everyone else."

"*Ya*, I get that. But I guess the question is—do you want to be?"

"Do I *want* to be in step with everyone else?" She should have been aggravated at his teasing, but the way he was looking at her caused her emotions to tumble here and there. They continued walking beside the creek, and she finally said, "Well, I'm not sure. What are you suggesting?"

Instead of continuing to tease her, Nick stopped. Since they were still holding hands, she bounced back like a yoyo connected by a string. Nick smiled, put his arms around her, then ducked his head and kissed her lips.

Wow! She felt chill bumps all the way to her toes.

"You're blushing."

"Well, *ya*. Kiss a girl like that and she's likely to blush."

Instead of letting her go, he waited for her to meet his gaze. "Do you want our relationship to become more permanent?"

"Our fake relationship?"

"*Nein.* You know very well that we're done with that. I'm speaking of our real relationship."

She heard Jacob and Joseph laughing and running toward them, but she didn't look away. She also didn't pretend, even to herself, that this moment wasn't very important. It was what she'd wanted, probably since he'd scolded her boys for catching Blue on the end of a hookless fishing line. It was what she'd dreamed of since the first time he'd kissed her. In that moment, she accepted the truth of how much Nick cared for her and how much she cared for him. And when she did that, the fears that she had so tightly clung to slipped away.

She wasn't unlovable.

She could trust her instincts—especially in regard to Nick.

She could allow herself to be happy.

"I'd like that very much."

"Me, too." He kissed her again, clasped her hand and they walked back toward the boys.

Chapter Fourteen

The next few weeks did not go as Nick hoped. John's health improved, then worsened, then improved again. The entire family pitched in to help with the work on the farm, but the bulk of it fell to Nick—mainly because he wanted to do it. He wanted to be there. He needed to be there.

But running two farms was no easy thing.

It was a Saturday, three weeks after John had the stents inserted, when Simon confronted him. Simon had come over from Middlebury on Friday to help with the harvest, as had the other siblings in the family. But it was Simon and Nick there at the end of the day, in the barn, doing the daily chores after a full day of harvest.

"How long do you think you can do this?"

"Do what?" Nick paused, pitchfork in hand, standing in the middle of Rhapsody's stall.

Simon was leaning against the opposite wall, arms crossed, hat tipped back. "How long do you think you can run two farms?"

"I'm not "

"You are. Don't think we haven't noticed. Don't think it's not appreciated, either, because it is. The truth of the matter is that *Dat*'s never going to be able to do these things again. We need to come up with a more permanent solution."

Nick swiped at the sweat dribbling down his face. He always did work up a sweat when he mucked out a stall, even when it was a cool October evening.

"About that…"

"*Ya?*"

But then he didn't know how to say it. He hadn't looked at his five-year plan in weeks. He couldn't envision how this was going to work out, but maybe he didn't need to depend on his five-year plan. He knew that asking Deborah to marry him was the right thing to do. He knew it was what he wanted to do. *Gotte* had placed him in this place at this time to care for Deborah and her family.

"The thing is that I'd like to ask Deborah to marry me."

"So, what are you waiting for?" The question held no condemnation, only amusement.

"I guess the perfect moment. The timing just feels— wrong."

"Ah, *ya*. I've heard of those perfect moments—the sun is dipping over a pristine field, your gal is by your side, maybe a redbird lands on a tree branch just at the edge of your vision. You hear a melodic song, and you know it's the perfect moment. You turn to the love of your life and ask her to be your *fraa*, and she says yes."

"Now you're making fun of me." He pointed the pitchfork at Simon, but he laughed with him. "Was that how it was with you and Mary? Sunsets and redbirds and all?"

"Hardly. Mary and I had been to an outing over in Middlebury. I guess the place we ate, the food must have been bad or something, because she was terribly sick for the next twenty-four hours. I went to her parents' home to check on her…" He shook his head at the memory. "I saw her in bed, all exhausted and sweating, and I knew… it was the perfect moment."

"Seriously?"

"Oh, *ya*. She puked before and after I asked her to be my *fraa*."

Nick laughed so hard that he had to press a hand to ease the stitch in his side. "You're making that up."

"I'm not." Simon joined him in the stall, and they quickly finished mucking it out and laying fresh hay. As they hung the tools on their hooks on the wall, he clasped Nick on the shoulder. "The important thing was that she said yes. That's what makes a perfect proposal, my friend. When both parties say yes."

Nick went to bed at his normal time, and he should have fallen right asleep. He didn't. Instead, he crossed his arms behind his head and stared up at the ceiling. Blue lay snoring softly on the rug. A slight breeze whispered through the open window.

He was an idiot.

Simon was right.

He didn't have to wait until he had the answer to every question about their future. They'd find those answers together. But Nick might be wrong about the proposal. Deborah deserved more than food poisoning and a puke bucket.

By the time he fell asleep, he had the perfect plan— or at least he thought it was the perfect plan.

The next day Nick and Deborah's *bruders* spent another four hours in the field, but then the harvest was done. John watched from a chair set out under the shade tree. Bethany sat beside him, shelling peas. Deborah helped with the harvest, as did her *schweschdern*. Her hair was covered with an old *kapp*, and she was wearing the same work dress she'd worn the day they'd gone kayaking. Was that the day he had well and truly fallen in love with her? He suspected it had happened even before that. Maybe it had even been the first day he'd met her.

He'd spent too much time struggling with those feelings. He was ready to accept them, to own them and to see where they led. He wanted Deborah and the twins in his life, for the rest of his life.

Jacob and Joseph were growing as fast as the corn they'd just harvested, though Joseph was beating Jacob by a fraction of an inch. Nick could now tell the two apart. He wondered that he'd ever had trouble with that. They might be twins, but they were two very different people. Joseph was quiet, thoughtful, a bit shy. Jacob was more impulsive, but he also had a commendable amount of energy.

A lump formed in his throat as he realized that both boys would probably have families of their own in fifteen years. Fifteen years. They would pass in the blink of an eye.

Everyone trooped back to the house for a late lunch. After they'd finished the meal, Nick motioned the boys outside and shared with them what he had in mind. He didn't tell them everything—he didn't tell them why he wanted to be alone with Deborah or what he was going to ask her, but he had a feeling that maybe they knew.

High-fiving his brother, Joseph declared, "I'll grab the picnic quilt and the sheets from the homework box."

"I know where the mason jars are." Jacob bounced from foot to foot. "I hope we can find the right kind of flowers."

"Anything will do. And boys…" Nick waited until they turned to look at him. *"Danki."*

They grinned again, then, instead of running to the house, they stepped closer and both gave him a tight hug. It brought tears to his eyes, but Nick wasn't embarrassed. Happiness that overflowed from your soul wasn't something to be self-conscious about. It was something to be grateful for, and he was.

The boys took off on their errands. Nick gave them thirty minutes, and then he went in search of Deborah.

He found her in the mudroom, rinsing out the dishcloths. "Care to go for a walk?"

"Sounds lovely, though sitting on the porch sounds even better."

"Oh, but—"

He didn't know how to finish that sentence. Deborah turned to study him. She laughed and wagged her finger at him. "Sounds like someone would like to go for a walk, though, so I'm all for it."

"Gut. Real *gut.* Well, I'll just…um… I need to go and speak with your *dat* first, and then I'll be ready."

"Okay. He's on the back porch." She nodded toward the double swing that they'd sat on together so many times. "I'll go with you."

"Nein!"

Now she looked at him as if he was wearing his suspenders backward.

"What I mean is, I have a hankering for some of those oatmeal cookies you made."

"After all the lunch you ate?"

"And maybe a thermos of coffee. That would hit the spot." He needed to buy himself five minutes, maybe ten. "I'll come and get you after I'm finished speaking with John."

"That sounds like a *wunderbaar* plan." She shook her head in amusement. "I'll go and make a pot of coffee."

Excellent. Coffee took a *gut* ten minutes to percolate.

He waited until she'd walked back into the kitchen, then he pushed through the screen door.

John smiled up at him when he sat down. "We appreciate your help, Nick."

"*Ya*, of course. No problem."

"We recognize all you've done around here these past few weeks. You've been a real blessing to me and to my family. *Gotte* knew what our needs would be when He prompted you to buy the farm next door."

Nick swallowed past the lump in his throat. He could hear Deborah and Mary talking in the kitchen. He was aware of a slight breeze stirring the bare tree limbs. He could smell coffee and cooking and autumn. It was as if every one of his senses was on hyperalert.

"Something on your mind, son?"

And that last word helped him over the hurdle of his insecurities. "I'd like to ask Deborah to marry me, but before I do…I'd like your blessing. That means a lot to me, John. It's important that you know how I feel about her, about the boys, about the entire family."

John smiled, but he didn't interrupt. He let Nick have the space to speak what was on his heart.

"Jacob and Joseph, they're amazing. And though they aren't my children in one sense, they will be in all the ways that matter. I care for them. I will pray for them every day. I already do, and I'll do my best to guide them—as you've guided your *kinner*."

Nick ran out of words there. He didn't know what else to say, how best to present his case. His house was too small, too old, and then there was the matter of the two farms.

But those were details that could be worked out.

What mattered was John's response and Deborah's answer.

John tapped his fingertips against the arm of the swing. "I believe you have loved this entire family since the day that you bought the goats…"

"And Jacob let them loose."

"And Deborah fell in the trough." John smiled, nodding his head at the memory. "You were aggravated at them, but I believe you were more aggravated at yourself because my family didn't fit into your future plans."

"My five-year plan."

"*Ya.* A family can mess with plans. Sometimes things take a turn in unexpected directions, but that's not what matters. What matters is that you can count on the fact that the people you love will be there for you and *Gotte* will provide."

"As far as the two farms—"

"Don't worry about that, Nick. We'll work it out."

"We will?"

"Together—after you ask Deborah, that is. And if she says yes."

"Do you think she will?" His plans for the future skidded to an abrupt stop. "Do you think she won't?"

"There's only one way to find out." But John's smile indicated his confidence that things would turn out the way that Nick hoped they would.

Deborah called from the door of the mudroom, "I have coffee and cookies. Anything else you need for this walk?"

"*Nein.* That sounds perfect."

At that point Jacob and Joseph appeared in front of the porch, waving wildly and giving him a thumbs-up sign. When Nick waved his thanks, they jogged off toward the front of the house. Blue dashed after them, hot on their heels.

John patted him on the back, and Nick stood and walked toward Deborah, toward the single person who mattered the most to him, and hopefully—toward his future.

Deborah was tired from the harvest. Traditionally, women did help in the fields—harvesttime was an all-hands-on-deck sort of activity. In addition, there was the usual cooking and cleaning to go along with the work in the fields. Her siblings had all shown up to help for the last two days, and of course Nick had been there.

She darted a peek in Nick's direction.

They were once again holding hands as they walked away from the house. He was up to something. She could tell it by the way he kept looking at her and then glancing away.

"Did you have a specific destination in mind?"

"*Ya.* I thought we'd sit by the pond for a spell."

"We should have invited Jacob and Joseph. In fact, where are the boys?"

"Oh, I think they…uh…had other things to do."

"Other things?"

"You know how they're always trying to teach Blue new tricks."

"They do love that dog. They're still pestering me about getting them one of their own."

Nick opened and closed his mouth.

"Do you think I should?"

"Oh, I don't know. They spend a lot of time with Blue. Just last week, Joseph taught him to sink onto his belly and then crawl backward. And Jacob is still convinced he can outrun the dog, though I've told him that blue heelers are cattle dogs. They're basically bred for speed and endurance. Some days it seems as if Blue is more their dog than mine."

He paused, and Deborah had that sense again that Nick was up to something. He glanced at her and then quickly looked away. And was he blushing?

She hoped something wasn't wrong. Dealing with her *dat*'s recuperation was enough pressure, not to mention the shenanigans Jacob and Joseph fell into on a daily basis. Deborah squeezed his hand. "You know you can tell me anything, right?"

"Oh, sure. *Ya.* You're a *gut* listener."

Hmm. That didn't work. There was definitely something on his mind, but he wasn't ready to spill it yet.

She supposed she'd find out soon enough, so she focused on breathing in the crisp fall air, enjoying the colors of the leaves they were walking through, listening to the birdsong. It was a *gut* day—a perfect day.

Then they rounded the corner toward the pond, and instead of sitting on the closest side, he led her around to the back.

As they walked toward it, she looked, stopped walking, looked again and shook her head in disbelief. She covered her mouth with her hand, but the laughter spilled through her fingers. "When did you have time to do this? A real picnic…"

He didn't answer. He pulled her toward the quilt Jacob and Joseph had placed under the bare limbs of a maple tree. As they drew closer, she saw half a dozen mason jars filled with clusters of wildflowers. Red, yellow and brown fall leaves had been sprinkled around the mason jars. Under one of the jars, someone had tucked two pieces of paper.

Nick set the thermos and container of cookies down

on the quilt, then tugged on her hand until they were standing in the middle of it. The quilt was an old, tattered one—something they often used for picnics. But how did Nick know about that?

"Let's sit."

"Okay."

When they were settled, he reached for the sheets of paper that were tucked under one of the mason jars. It was only then that she realized what they were—Jacob's drawing. Joseph's story. She took them from his hands, staring first at the drawing. She ran her finger across each person—her *mamm*, *dat*, herself, Jacob, Joseph and Nick. They were all stick figures, their stick-figure hands connected to one another. They all had huge smiles on their faces, and a stick dog—Blue, no doubt—stuck his head out between the two boys. They stood in a line, a tree next to them and the pond off to the right.

She looked at Nick, who had been silent, studying her, waiting. "It's the same spot."

"It is."

"Did you do this? The flowers and the quilt and... this?" She held up the sheets of paper.

"*Nein.* Jacob and Joseph did."

She looked at the second sheet. Joseph's title at the top in bold, heavy letters read *My Family*. A few lines jumped out at her.

Our neighbor Nick...

Blue is the best.

We're like a family.

Nick scooted closer, so that they were sitting knee to knee, like two teenagers with their legs crossed and their faces mere inches apart. His voice, when he spoke, was soft and low and choked with emotion. "I wanted a private moment with you, Deborah, but I also wanted the boys to be a part of it."

Now her thoughts were swimming. She heard his words, saw the tender look on his face, but she couldn't quite make sense of what was happening. She put down the sheets of paper, carefully setting them back under the mason jar so they wouldn't blow away, and she noticed that her arms were shaking.

Then Nick reached for both of her hands, held them tenderly in his, and her shaking stopped.

"I love you very much, Deborah."

"You love me?"

"I do."

"I love you, too." She didn't even have to think about it. The words felt like a natural extension of everything she carried in her heart.

"I brought you out here because I wanted a special place to ask you to marry me."

"Marry you?"

"I wanted you to know that I'm not just asking you. I'm asking Jacob and Joseph, too, if they're willing to be a family. It seems to me, though..." He nodded at the papers. "It seems that they've already answered that question. Maybe they understood what was happening before I did."

"You're asking me to marry you?"

"*Ya*. I am." He looked as if he wanted to say more, but he didn't. Instead, he stopped and waited. He gave her a moment to gather her thoughts.

But Deborah didn't need any more time to think. She'd been thinking about this—dreaming about it— for some time now.

"Yes."

"Yes?" He looked surprised.

She laughed. "Did you expect me to say no?"

"Yes!" He jumped up, let out a whoop, turned in a circle, then dropped back down beside her. "We're going to be married."

"Yes, we are."

It was then that he cradled her face in his hands, moved toward her and kissed her lips.

In that kiss, Deborah felt his love for her. She felt his confidence in their future together, and his promise to be by her side. Could a single kiss hold that much? She thought maybe it could. She thought this kiss did.

They sat there another hour, talking about their future, enjoying the cookies and coffee. Finally, the boys, unable to contain their curiosity any longer, jogged toward them, Blue loping at their side.

Deborah had recovered from her surprise.

The world was no longer tilting.

In fact, she'd never felt on more solid ground.

"Nick has a question for you two."

Both boys dropped onto the quilt. Their red heads and freckles and earnest expressions tugged on Deborah's heartstrings as they always did. And this man sitting with them, he seemed part of a painting of their life— like Jacob's drawing and Joseph's story.

"Did we do *gut* with the flowers?" Joseph asked.

"Were you two kissing?" Jacob made a horrified look, and everyone laughed.

"You both did a *wunderbaar* job. I picked this special place…"

"It's the place in my picture!" Jacob had been staring down at the sheet, and now he looked around in surprise. "I draw pretty *gut*."

"And I write pretty *gut*." Joseph looked up from rereading his story. In the traditional Joseph way, he looked more serious than his *bruder*, as if he was waiting for something important.

"I picked this place because I wanted somewhere special to ask your *mamm* to marry me."

Jacob and Joseph exchanged a look, then turned their attention to Deborah.

"What did you say?" Jacob asked.

Joseph tightened his grip on the sheet of paper. "Did you say yes?"

"I did." Deborah felt tears prick her eyes for the first time. Why would she cry now? Her heart, her dreams, were one thing, but oh, how she loved these two boys. Their dreams were even more important than her own. "I did, and that means we'll be a family—like in your drawing, Jacob. And in your writing, Joseph."

"We want you to know that you're an important part of this decision," Nick clarified. "I guess what I'm saying is… I'd like to be your *dat*, if that's okay."

For their answer, both boys launched themselves into Nick's arms. And it was when Deborah saw that, when she saw the man she loved holding the boys who meant so much to her, that tears slipped down Deborah's face.

"Don't cry, *Mamm*." Joseph shifted to sit beside her. "This is a *gut* thing."

"*Ya*, it is." Jacob turned his attention to Blue, who had dropped down onto the quilt beside them. "Hear that, Blue? You're going to be our dog."

And then both boys were on their feet. Jacob pulled a ball from his pocket. He threw it, and Joseph and Blue took off running, Jacob only a few steps behind.

Deborah and Nick stood, then moved off the old quilt. She reached for the blanket, began to fold it, but Nick took it from her and set it down on the ground, next to the mason jars. He turned her to face the pond and beyond that the boys and the house. He stood behind her, his arms around her, and pulled her close.

"I love you, Deborah."

"I love you, Nick." She tilted her head back to look at him. "This is going to throw a lot of kinks into your five-year plan."

"Indeed, it is."

Now she spun in his arms, touched his face and softly kissed his lips. Foreheads touching, she whispered, "And to think it all started with fake dating."

"Best idea you ever had."

"My boys can be a lot of trouble," she admitted.

"Double trouble."

Then he laughed, and she did, too. As the fall sun tilted toward the western horizon, covering the land with golden rays, they walked back toward home, following the dog and the two boys. It seemed to Deborah that together—as a family—they were walking into their future.

Epilogue

A workday was scheduled in March, and Nick's home was gutted, then rebuilt. It was done ahead of his five-year plan. It was done for his family.

The wedding took place on a beautiful April afternoon. The weather allowed for an outdoor celebration that was held at Deborah's parents' farm, back by the pond—the very same place that Nick had asked her to marry him. The same place that Jacob and Joseph had described in their schoolwork.

Deborah wore a pale green dress.

Nick wore black pants and a new white shirt.

Jacob and Joseph sported new hats as well as their Sunday best clothes. Jacob had a spot of mud on his pants that Deborah pretended not to notice. Joseph kept straightening his suspenders.

Someone had even thought to bathe Blue.

Bishop Ezekiel smiled at the boys and the dog, who sat in the front row. Then he turned his attention to Deborah and Nick.

"Do you, Nick Stoltzfus, and you, Deborah Mast, vow to remain together until death?"

"We do," they said in unison.

"And will you both be loyal and care for each other... even during, especially during, times of adversity?"

"We will."

"And during affliction?"

"Yes."

"And during sickness?"

"We've already done all that," Jacob muttered to Joseph, who hushed him.

Nick's smile grew even wider, and Deborah felt as if her heart literally hurt from the joy and importance of the moment.

"We will," they both said.

Ezekiel carefully shut his Bible, running a weathered hand over the well-worn cover. Then he tucked it under his arm, and reached out for Deborah and Nick. He placed his hand over theirs.

"All of your neighbors, *freinden* and family gathered here today will pray for you and your marriage and your family. As your bishop and friend, I will pray for you. We all wish you the blessing and mercy of *Gotte*."

He turned them gently to face the crowd.

Deborah looked out through tear-filled eyes. The day had been perfect.

And then Blue caught sight of Oliver. The cat hissed. The dog barked. Joseph threw himself at the dog, but Blue was too fast. Joseph landed on the ground, Jacob helped his *bruder* up, and after looking for permission from their *mamm*, they chased after the dog. Oliver sat primly, cleaning his face.

Nick stepped closer and whispered, "I suspect we will have few boring moments in this family."

"And you're okay with that?"

"I am. In fact, boring is overrated." He intertwined his fingers with hers, and together they walked into the embrace of their friends and family.

* * * * *

If you loved this story,
pick up the other books in the
Indiana Amish Brides series
from bestselling author
Vannetta Chapman

A Widow's Hope
Amish Christmas Memories
A Perfect Amish Match
The Amish Christmas Matchmaker
An Unlikely Amish Match
The Amish Christmas Secret
The Baby Next Door
An Amish Baby for Christmas

Available now from Love Inspired!
Find more great reads at www.LoveInspired.com

Dear Reader,

Have you ever made a mistake that you thought there was no recovering from? Sometimes it's hard to seek the forgiveness of others. Sometimes it's even harder to forgive yourself.

Deborah Mast is a single mom of twin boys. She's not sure she believes in happily-ever-after, and she has no idea how to move past the mistakes she's made. Nicholas Stoltzfus has experienced his share of heartache. His plan is to focus on being a good farmer. His plan is to go it alone.

But God has brought Deborah and Nick together for a reason. The question is whether they'll be brave enough to give God's plan a chance.

I hope you enjoyed reading *The Amish Twins Next Door*. I welcome comments and letters at vannettachapman @gmail.com.

May we continue to give "thanks always for all things unto God and the Father in the name of our Lord Jesus Christ" (Ephesians 5:20).

Blessings,
Vannetta

LOVE INSPIRED

Stories to uplift and inspire

Fall in love with Love Inspired—
inspirational and uplifting stories of faith
and hope. Find strength and comfort in
the bonds of friendship and community.
Revel in the warmth of possibility and the
promise of new beginnings.

Sign up for the Love Inspired newsletter
at **LoveInspired.com** to be the first
to find out about upcoming titles,
special promotions and exclusive content.

CONNECT WITH US AT:

Facebook.com/LoveInspiredBooks

Twitter.com/LoveInspiredBks

COMING NEXT MONTH FROM
Love Inspired

THE AMISH MATCHMAKER'S CHOICE
Redemption's Amish Legacies • by Patricia Johns
Newly returned to the Amish community, Jake Knussli must find a wife in six months or lose his uncle's farm. Can matchmaker Adel Draschel secure a *frau* for him—before losing her own heart to the handsome farmer?

THEIR PRETEND COURTSHIP
The Amish of New Hope • by Carrie Lighte
Pressured by her stepfather to court, Eliza Keim begrudgingly walks out with blueberry farmer Jonas Kanagy—except Jonas is only trying to protect his brother from what he thinks are Eliza's heartbreaker ways. When the two are forced to make their courtship in name only look real, they may discover more than they bargained for...

GUARDING HIS SECRET
K-9 Companions • by Jill Kemerer
When Wyoming rancher Randy Watkins finds himself caring for his surprise baby nephew, he seeks the help of longtime friend Hannah Carr. But when her retired service dog seems to sense all is not right with Randy's health, will he trust Hannah with the truth?

THE RANCHER'S FAMILY LEGACY
The Ranchers of Gabriel Bend • by Myra Johnson
Building contractor Mark Caldwell is ready to inherit his grandfather's horse ranch and put his traumatic past behind him—if he can survive working in Texas Hill Country for a year. But when his dog bonds with local caterer Holly Elliot's son, can they put aside their differences and open their hearts?

HER MOUNTAIN REFUGE
by Laurel Blount
Widowed, pregnant and under the thumb of her controlling mother-in-law, Charlotte Tremaine needs help—but she doesn't expect it to come from her estranged childhood best friend. Yet letting Sheriff Logan Carter whisk her away to his foster mother's remote mountain home might be her best chance at a fresh start...

A MOTHER FOR HIS SON
by Betty Woods
In town to help her grandmother, chef Rachel Landry plans to use the time to heal her broken heart—not help Mac Greer with his guest ranch. But her growing affection for his little boy could be just the push she needs to once again see the possibility of something more...

LOOK FOR THESE AND OTHER LOVE INSPIRED BOOKS WHEREVER BOOKS ARE SOLD, INCLUDING MOST BOOKSTORES, SUPERMARKETS, DISCOUNT STORES AND DRUGSTORES.

LICNM0422

Get 4 FREE REWARDS!

We'll send you 2 FREE Books plus 2 FREE Mystery Gifts.

FREE Value Over **$20**

Both the **Love Inspired®** and **Love Inspired® Suspense** series feature compelling novels filled with inspirational romance, faith, forgiveness, and hope.

YES! Please send me 2 FREE novels from the Love Inspired or Love Inspired Suspense series and my 2 FREE gifts (gifts are worth about $10 retail). After receiving them, if I don't wish to receive any more books, I can return the shipping statement marked "cancel." If I don't cancel, I will receive 6 brand-new Love Inspired Larger-Print books or Love Inspired Suspense Larger-Print books every month and be billed just $5.99 each in the U.S. or $6.24 each in Canada. That is a savings of at least 17% off the cover price. It's quite a bargain! Shipping and handling is just 50¢ per book in the U.S. and $1.25 per book in Canada.* I understand that accepting the 2 free books and gifts places me under no obligation to buy anything. I can always return a shipment and cancel at any time. The free books and gifts are mine to keep no matter what I decide.

Choose one: ☐ **Love Inspired Larger-Print** (122/322 IDN GNWC) ☐ **Love Inspired Suspense Larger-Print** (107/307 IDN GNWN)

Name (please print)

Address   Apt. #

City   State/Province   Zip/Postal Code

Email: Please check this box ☐ if you would like to receive newsletters and promotional emails from Harlequin Enterprises ULC and its affiliates. You can unsubscribe anytime.

Mail to the **Harlequin Reader Service:**
IN U.S.A.: P.O. Box 1341, Buffalo, NY 14240-8531
IN CANADA: P.O. Box 603, Fort Erie, Ontario L2A 5X3

Want to try 2 free books from another series! Call 1-800-873-8635 or visit www.ReaderService.com.

---

*Terms and prices subject to change without notice. Prices do not include sales taxes, which will be charged (if applicable) based on your state or country of residence. Canadian residents will be charged applicable taxes. Offer not valid in Quebec. This offer is limited to one order per household. Books received may not be as shown. Not valid for current subscribers to the Love Inspired or Love Inspired Suspense series. All orders subject to approval. Credit or debit balances in a customer's account(s) may be offset by any other outstanding balance owed by or to the customer. Please allow 4 to 6 weeks for delivery. Offer available while quantities last.

Your Privacy—Your information is being collected by Harlequin Enterprises ULC, operating as Harlequin Reader Service. For a complete summary of the information we collect, how we use this information and to whom it is disclosed, please visit our privacy notice located at corporate.harlequin.com/privacy-notice. From time to time we may also exchange your personal information with reputable third parties. If you wish to opt out of this sharing of your personal information, please visit readerservice.com/consumerchoice or call 1-800-873-8635. **Notice to California Residents**—Under California law, you have specific rights to control and access your data. For more information on these rights and how to exercise them, visit corporate.harlequin.com/california-privacy.

LIRLIS22

"What do I need to know?" Hannah faced him then, her big blue eyes full of expectation. Randy liked that about her. She didn't hide anything.

Well, everyone hid something. He'd certainly been hiding something for years—from this town, from his friends, even from his brother.

So what? It was nobody's business.

"Let's start with the basics." He gave her a quick tour. Her presence was making his pulse race. He didn't like it or the reason why it was happening.

Hannah's cell phone rang. "Do you mind if I take this?"

"Go ahead." He backed up to give her privacy, busying himself with a box of nets, but he could hear every word she said.

"You're kidding," she said breathlessly. "That's great news. Yes…Right now? I'd love to…You're serious? I can't believe it…"

Finally, she ended the conversation and turned to him with shining eyes. "That was Molly. She has a dog for me."

"Another puppy?" He placed the box on the counter.

"No, a retired service dog." She looked ready to float through the air. "I've been on the adoption list forever. The ones that have become available all went to either their original puppy raiser or someone higher on the list."

"Won't the dog be old?" Why would she want someone's ancient dog that might not live long?

"Some of them are. This one is eight. Too old to be placed for service, but he's still got a lot of good years left."

Something told him that even if the dog had only a couple of good months left, Hannah would be equally enthusiastic.

"I'm going to go pick him up." She lightly clapped her hands in happiness, and he kind of wished he could go with her.

"Let me get you the store key, then."

"Oh, wait." She winced. "I didn't think this through. Is there any way I can bring him with me to the store? He passed all of his obedience classes years ago. I'm sure he wouldn't cause any trouble. I just can't imagine bringing him home and then leaving him by himself all day before he has a chance to get to know me. He's used to being with someone all the time."

"Of course. Bring him." He'd always liked dogs. His customers wouldn't mind. In fact, they'd probably linger in the store even more because of him. Maybe he'd get a dog of his own after he moved into the new house. It was a thought.

"Thanks." She came over and gave him a quick hug. "I'll open the store tomorrow at nine. You're closed on Sundays, right?"

"Right." He stood frozen from the shock of her touch as she hurried to the back. The sound of the screen door slamming jolted him out of his stupor.

Hannah almost made him forget he wasn't like any other guy.

And he wasn't.

He had a secret. And that secret would stay with him until the day he died.

When that day came, he'd be single.

He had to be more careful around Hannah Carr. There was something about her that made his logic disappear like the morning dew. He couldn't afford to forget he couldn't have her.

Don't miss Guarding His Secret
by Jill Kemerer, available June 2022
wherever Love Inspired books and ebooks are sold.

LoveInspired.com

IF YOU ENJOYED THIS BOOK, DON'T MISS NEW EXTENDED-LENGTH NOVELS FROM LOVE INSPIRED!

In addition to the Love Inspired books you know and love, we're excited to introduce even more uplifting stories in a longer format, with more inspiring fresh starts and page-turning thrills!

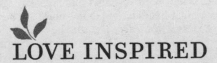

Stories to uplift and inspire.

Fall in love with Love Inspired—inspirational and uplifting stories of faith and hope. Find strength and comfort in the bonds of friendship and community. Revel in the warmth of possibility, and the promise of new beginnings.

LOOK FOR THESE LOVE INSPIRED TITLES ONLINE AND IN THE BOOK DEPARTMENT OF YOUR FAVORITE RETAILER!

LITRADE0422